# THE
# DEATH-CAP
# DANCERS

# THE DEATH-CAP DANCERS

## *Gladys Mitchell*

ST. MARTIN'S PRESS
NEW YORK

Library of Congress Cataloging in Publication Data

Mitchell, Gladys, 1901-
    The death-cap dancers.

    I. Title.
PR6025.I832D4    1981        823'.912        81-14519
ISBN -0-312-18608-8                          AACR2

# Contents

To the long life and happiness of
ADRIAN STEWART SHERATON,
born on St. George's Day, 1979

'. . . . . for thou art much too fair
To be death's conquest and make worms thine heir.'
*William Shakespeare*
Sonnet VI

# — 1 —

# WOOD PIMPERNEL

Hermione Lestrange — Hermy One to her intimates — stopped the car, got out and surveyed her surroundings. For the last two or three miles she had been uneasily aware that in taking what she had hoped would be a short cut as well as serving to take her off the main road for twenty miles or so, she must have misread the map and was now in a wilderness of cotton-grass, peat-bogs and heather.

She was on an unfenced moorland track which rose and dipped with the undulations of the landscape, bending away in a direction which she was certain could not be the one she wanted.

She had pulled up at a solitary signpost which to her slightly disordered mind represented nothing so much as a gibbet. It had only one arm and this pointed along an even narrower road than the one she was on and read, tersely and unhelpfully, *Wayland Only*.

'Thanks a lot,' said Hermione aloud. All round her were the Yorkshire moors on their high plateau. In the far distance she could make out a line of blue hills. The autumn evening was coming on and there were pockets of mist in the dips and hollows. The road she was travelling seemed to go on for ever, losing itself on the downward slopes and appearing again on the rising ground beyond them.

She had two chances, as she saw the situation. One was to push on in the hope of striking the main road after all; the other was to reverse the car, return to the little town of Gledge End on whose outskirts she had turned off on to the moors and begin again from there.

Whatever she did she was unlikely to reach her destination until after dark. She was an adventurous soul, but the thought of being benighted on the moors was enough to daunt the stoutest hearted, so she was about to take the sensible course and reverse the car when she was aware of three women emerging from a dip in the moor. Two of them were giving the third a 'bandy-chair'.

When they saw Hermione and the car the two supporters dumped their burden in the heather and one of them remained beside her while the other ran forward waving her arms. With sinking heart Hermione realised that she was going to be asked to give the three women a lift and she knew that in such a place and at such a time of day there was no way in which her conscience could allow her to refuse such a request.

It was an uphill run to where Hermione was standing and the woman was panting as she came near. She was wearing a yellow woollen cap surmounted by a pom-pom, jeans, a sweater and an anorak and appeared to be about thirty years old.

'Oh, I say, you've got a car,' she said. 'If there's anything of the Good Samaritan about you, would you — *could* you — give us a lift? My idiot sister has wrenched her ankle and I don't think we can possibly carry her home.'

'I've got to do another eighty miles or so, and I've lost my way,' said Hermione. 'I was just going to turn the car and go back to Gledge End. I could take you that far if it would be any good.'

The woman looked back at the other two. The one in the heather was being hauled to her feet. Clutching her companion, she hobbled a step or two and then sank down again.

'Gledge End would be better than nothing,' said the woman to Hermione. 'I daresay we could hire a car from there. Actually where we are staying would be on your way, give or take half a mile or so. Look, we really are in a bit of a spot. Couldn't you stretch a point for once? Honestly, it would hardly take you out of your way at all, and we really would be damned grateful.'

Mist in the hollows of the moor was rising higher and thickening. There was a dank smell of autumn in the air, the smell of damp, dead bracken and dying heather. A wind had got up and the darkening evening was chilly.

'Get in,' said Hermione. 'The back seat, perhaps, and then the injured ankle can slide in beside me when we pick her up. I'll run you home and book in at Gledge End. I shall never get to my aunt's tonight. What do I do when we've picked up the other two?'

'Reverse and then take that turning to Wayland. We've got a cabin in Wayland Forest. Only took it over this morning and now this has to happen.'

The woman who had remained with the unfortunate casualty appeared to be of about the same age as the one who had waylaid Hermione. The victim was younger and Hermione surmised that she was a contemporary of her own.

The Wayland turning began to leave the moors behind. The first indication that they were entering the forest was that the wayside verges had become wide stretches of rough grass instead of heather. Beyond them, on the right, was a plantation of young conifers and on the left a thick, densely populated wood of mature trees. The car was on the outskirts of Forestry Commission property.

'Did you say you might stay in Gledge End for the night?' asked the woman who had asked for a lift. 'Do you know somebody there?'

'No, but there are hotels. They won't be full at this time of year.'

'Oh, but why bother with hotels? We can put you up for the night if you don't mind a bunk bed and a continental quilt to cover you.'

'I shall have to telephone my aunt.'

'Nothing easier. There's a call-box at the warden's office and a carpark where it's perfectly safe to leave the car.'

'I can't wish myself on you like that.'

'Why on earth not? We seem to have wished ourselves on to you and your car all right. There are just the three of us and the cabin sleeps six. Do stay. We'd love to have you. I'm Isobel Lindsay and the lunatic cripple beside you is my sister Tamsin. The silent member of the party is Erica Lyndhurst, with whom I was at school.'

'I'm not so silent that I can't say thank you,' said Erica Lyndhurst. 'We're very grateful, I can tell you, and we'll be delighted to put you up after you've telephoned your folks.'

'Do you have a name?' asked Hermione's seat-mate, the girl with the wrenched ankle. 'I hardly dare open my mouth to ask because I'm well and truly in the doghouse, but I couldn't help twisting my ankle. A grouse got up almost under my feet and I was so startled that I stepped back and my foot went into a hole.'

'I'm Hermione Lestrange.'

'Benenden, Roedean or Cheltenham Ladies' College?' enquired Isobel, who seemed to be the liveliest of the three.

'Remand home, approved school and Holloway Gaol, if you *must* know,' said Hermione, who was feeling more cheerful.

'Our kind of woman, in fact,' said Isobel. 'But let us sort out the subordinate clauses. The name Lestrange rings a warning bell, although I expect I'm on the wrong platform. I attended a lecture given by an eminent psychiatrist called Dame Beatrice Lestrange Bradley and was much impressed. She was speaking about the problems of the one-parent family and when it came to question time I was determined to get in on the act, so I said that in my experience — I'm a schoolmistress, as you may have deduced — many of the children who came from one-parent families (mostly when the parent was a widow) were, I had to admit, far better behaved than those from many of the families where there were two parents. I asked her to explain this.'

'But it's not always true,' said Tamsin.

'I never said it was. I said it was true of many families.'

'What was her answer?' asked Hermione.

'She said that enlightened mums expected good conduct, and therefore stood a good chance of getting it. She asked whether that didn't apply to classroom discipline, too, and, of course, it does. She then referred me to the famous speech made by Gussie Fink-Nottle to the boys of Market Snodsbury Grammar School in which, quoting, no doubt, from a higher authority, he had assured the lads that education was a drawing-out, not a putting-in. She then reminded me that Mr Fink-Nottle was strongly under the influence of alcohol at the time, and hoped that she had answered my question to my satisfaction.'

'It sounds typical of my great-aunt. The Delphic Oracle could have taken her correspondence course. I often think she ought to have gone in for politics. Personally I am the complete dumb-cluck of the family. I help my father on his pig-farm.'

'I'm a painter of pot-boilers,' said Tamsin, 'and I hope this ankle isn't going to be a perishing nuisance because I want to spend the next fortnight painting the forest and the moors.'

'Well, you haven't broken it, anyway,' said Erica. 'I'll strap it up for you when we get back. I'm always dealing with minor accidents on the site.'

'Erica's father is a builder and surveyor,' said Isobel, 'and she's stinking rich. She only bothers to know us because I was at school with her.'

'I act as my father's accounts clerk and general dogsbody,' explained Erica, 'and now he's made me a partner. Our work slackens from now until the spring, so I thought I'd take a couple of weeks off. These two girls make a change, I must say, from a world of rough, hearty, booze-swilling workmen, much as I love 'em.'

'Tamsin can get away any time she wants,' said Isobel, 'on the pretence of finding something to paint.'

'Christmas and birthday-card subjects and, on commission, people's dogs and horses,' said Tamsin. 'Any chance your father would commission a picture of his pet pig?'

'Whereas I,' continued Isobel, 'am tied to school holidays. This time they've extended the usual half-term break from a week to a fortnight to conserve the winter fuel, so that accounts for my stabilising presence among you all.'

'I suppose the four of us make a pretty good cross-section,' said Erica. 'We represent the land, commerce, education and the arts.'

'Pigs, houses, schools and daubs,' said Tamsin. 'You three

have your uses, I suppose, but what about me?'

'At least you found a means to get us a lift home,' said her sister, 'and for that I am truly thankful. We went much further than we intended,' she added, speaking to Hermione, 'so her wretched ankle actually came in useful.'

The car began a long gradual descent and picked up a sandy road bordered by deciduous trees with a group here and there of Scots pines. Soon Hermione obtained a glimpse of wooden cabins half-hidden among the trees. Occasionally the car, which was now doing only about twenty miles an hour, passed little groups of walkers.

Under Tamsin's directions, Hermione at last pulled up in a large gravelled carpark not far from a complex of buildings which included a public call-box.

'Have you change for the phone?' asked Erica, whom Hermione was soon to recognise as the unofficial mother to the party.

'Oh, yes, thanks. I won't be long'. The result of the telephone call was unexpected. One of her aunts answered it and there was evident relief at that end of the line.

'Thank goodness you phoned! We've been on to Stanton St John, but, of course, you had left. My dear, of all things, the maid has got mumps, so, of course, you mustn't come anywhere near us at present. Your mother says you haven't had it and it can be serious at your age. So glad you've found somewhere to stay the night. We must fix up your visit for another time. *So* glad you are able to ring.'

'O.K.?' asked Isobel, when Hermione returned to the car. 'We really ought to walk to our cabin from here, but the ankle had better be taken up to the door. We'll get Tamsin indoors, then perhaps you'll bring me back here where you have to leave the car, and you and I can then walk back together.'

'What are all these buildings?'

'The warden's office and flat, a big lounge for the cabin people if they want a get-together, a television room, a playroom for the kids if the weather turns wet, a shop where we get our milk and newspapers and any oddments we run short of, a badminton court, a billiards room — you name it, it's here.'

Hermione backed the car and, again directed by Tamsin, drove to the cabin which the three women had rented.

'We're rather on the outskirts, in a way,' said Isobel, 'although not far from the carpark, thank goodness. There is only one other cabin opposite ours, and even that you can only see through the trees. We don't know what the people are like. We only came down today. Oh, well, here we are. Our home sweet home for a fortnight.'

Wooden steps led up to the front door of the cabin, and the structure itself seemed to be completely made of wood. Leaving Tamsin standing on one leg with Isobel supporting her, Erica unlocked the door and the three of them disappeared inside. Hermione unlocked the boot of the car and took out her own two suitcases which she put down at the foot of the steps. Erica came out again with Isobel and they picked up the suitcases and took them inside. Isobel rejoined Hermione and they drove to the carpark, left the car and then walked back among the trees.

It was not yet dark, but the number of leaves still on the trees made it shadowy in the woods. There were fallen leaves and pine-needles on the ground and miry patches in places along the walk. The air was fresh but not cold, and as they walked the few hundred yards which separated the carpark from the cabin, Hermione began to wish that she were staying.

The same thing appeared to be in Isobel's mind. She asked what Hermione proposed to do now that she could not go to her relatives.

'Go home, I suppose,' said Hermione.

'Why don't you stay with us? The cabin is supposed to sleep six and there are only the three of us at present. Don't make up your mind until you've seen what it's like, but I'm sure we'd be glad to have you if you cared to muck in.'

Lights were on in the cabin when they reached it. Tamsin, her ankle strapped up, was lying on a settee in the living quarters and Erica was in the kitchen preparing a meal. Isobel showed Hermione round the neat, well-ordered little holiday dwelling. It consisted of a lounge containing a settee, armchairs and a large dining table with benches, and there was a radiator for warmth. Opening off the lounge were the two bedrooms, a kitchenette and a shower-room. One bedroom had a double and a single bed in it and a settee which could be turned into another bed. The smaller room contained two bunks, one of which had to be reached by means of a vertical ladder. There were two entrances to the cabin. The one by which Hermione had been brought in opened into a vestibule where coats, outdoors shoes, wellington boots and waterproofs could be left and in it there was another radiator to assist in the drying of wet clothes.

There were drawers, cupboards, wardrobes and shelves in every part of the cabin, but all were arranged as neatly and in as space-saving a manner as they would have been in an up-to-date and well-equipped caravan.

In contrast to the somewhat primitive appearance of the outside of the cabin, the inside walls were of shining, smooth, polished panelling. Outside the back entrance, which was by way of sliding french doors, there was a verandah with a table and benches for *al fresco* meals.

'It's a bit of a nuisance that all the mod con is in one room,' said Isobel, 'but I suppose to separate the mod from the con would be too much to ask. Otherwise we approve of the set-up. Yours is the top bunk, unless you've got no head for heights. Erica has bagged the big bed and Tamsin is to have the single, so, if you have an objection to the top bunk, the settee is available.'

'Supper up! Come and get it,' said Erica.

No objection was raised by anybody when Erica suggested bed at ten. Hermione, in the top bunk, woke early the next morning. The windows were high up in the wall and from where she was she could see the forest tree-tops. The windows did not open, but the bunkroom was supplied with the necessary ventilation through airholes also high up on the wall. She learned by her watch that it was almost seven o'clock. The sky would have paled sufficiently, she decided, for a before-breakfast walk. She felt for the top of her ladder and descended cautiously, without disturbing Isobel.

She picked up an armful of clothes, sneaked out into the

lounge, promised herself a shower when she got back, dressed and went out on to the verandah. Everything was quiet. Out on the moor on the previous evening there had been a wind, although it had not dispersed the rising mist, but here in the forest the silence was like that of an empty cathedral.

The stars were still faintly visible. She could see them caught up among the dark branches of the trees. The air was cold and sweet and she thought she could smell the pines. She stood for a few moments breathing in their aroma, then she descended the steps, crossed a rough patch of grass and found a path which was nothing more than a forest track. It glimmered pale, secretive and seductive in the almost no-light and looked, to her romantic imagination, like the legendary road to elf-land.

'And see ye not yon bonny road that winds about the ferny brae?' she said to herself as she followed it into the woods. Soon a dawn wind began to rustle the leaves which were still on the trees, and the sky lightened. The path widened and grew whiter. She followed its curves and gentle gradients, walking sometimes on its hard core, sometimes scuffling her feet with childlike pleasure through heaps of fallen leaves. The bushes took on a more familiar look and when she emerged into a clearing she could see the morning mist rising among the tree-trunks. A sharp autumn nip was now in the air and among the unkempt grasses and on the creeping trails of blackberry suckers which intruded on to the road were fine-spun, dew-wet, delicate cobwebs.

Hermione walked on, experiencing a kind of soul-filling delight. The light broadened, the mists began to disperse and she realised that it was time to turn back. When she re-entered the cabin Erica was already getting the breakfast.

'The others are still hogging it,' she said, 'so I'll just do enough for you and me and then they can get their own. I began to think you'd cut your stick'

·'And vanished, like the tart in the sea-shanty? Oh, no. I simply went for a walk.'

'What time do you want to leave?'

'I don't really want to leave at all. I've been in the woods, and it was marvellous.'

'How long were you going to stay with your aunt?'

'A fortnight, I suppose.'

'Well, you seem to be our sort. Why don't you stay with us?'

'Do you really think I could stay? Isobel did mention it last night.'

'Why not? The bed is there and you can pay for your food, I suppose. You'll have to take your share in doing the chores. We're not going to spoil you.' She gave Hermione a friendly smile and added, 'So there it is. Take it or leave it.'

# −2−

# WOOD SAGE

'I'll take it. I'd love to stay, so long as it's all right with the others.'

'You said Isobel mentioned it, and I'm sure Tamsin will agree, not that we take any notice of her as a general rule. If you want a shower, better have it now while the coast is clear before the others get up. I'll give you your breakfast as soon as you're through. I expect I'd better make some sort of rota. Four people to one shower-room need organising.'

'Are you a born organiser?'

'I've had organising thrust upon me from an early age. My mother died when I was eight and my father has not married again. Wonder whether there's a chance of getting the Sunday papers? We shall all want to sit about a bit after breakfast.'

At ten there was a caller. A tall young man was at the door when Erica answered it. He gave her a brisk greeting and added, 'I saw the boy cycling towards the shop with the papers. I'm going down for ours, so I wondered whether you'd like me to bring one for you. My name's John Trent. My parents and I have the cabin opposite yours.'

Isobel and Tamsin had breakfasted and it was Isobel who answered: 'Oh, thanks very much. *Sunday Times* and *Sunday Express*, if they've got them.'

'They had them last week.'

'You've been here a week, then?'

'Yes. Let me warn you to expect one of the foresters this morning.'

'Oh, Lord! What have we done?'

'Oh, nothing. It's simply that on the first Sunday morning a forester collects up the new arrivals and takes them on a conducted tour so that they know their way around. It's quite easy to get lost in the forest, although I should think the literature they supply and their map of the forest walks would be sufficient guide to anyone of average intelligence.'

'Ah, but not many people *are* of average intelligence,' said Isobel, 'as you would know if you had my job.'

'Even with average intelligence, you'd need a compass as well as a map,' said Tamsin from the settee. John Trent looked at the strapped-up ankle.

'So *you* won't be going on the pious pilgrimage,' he said.

'Not today, but it's only a wrench. I shall go out for a drive this afternoon, I expect.'

The forester, with another group of holiday-makers, turned up soon after John returned with the papers. Erica volunteered to keep Tamsin company and to cook the Sunday lunch while Isobel and Hermione went off with the party for a nominal half-hour's tour.

The suggested half-hour's walk turned into a protracted hike which lasted until lunchtime, for the forester was an enthusiastic naturalist and spared neither their ears nor their legs as he took them round. The party was given the names of trees and shrubs, and was taken out of the forest itself to be shown two species of amphibians, the common and the great crested newt, which had chosen to breed in an abandoned sheep-trough. Back in the forest they saw fungi, including the scabrous-looking orange phlebia sprouting from the dead bough of a forest oak — 'you can find it on birch, alder and gorse at any time of year' — and were shown the 'lawyer's wig', edible when young. 'We use it as an ingredient of a ketchup made with vinegar, salt, peppercorns, coriander and a touch of ground cloves. When the fungi are old they turn to a black mess which can be used as ink. And here we have . . .'

He became almost tiresomely informative and in the middle of a pine-wood and a dissertation on the red milk-cap which was spreading itself freely on the ground under the odiferous, tall, straight pine-trees, Isobel touched Hermione's arm and they sidled away and went back to the cabin.

'Did you enjoy it?' asked Tamsin.

'We were shown a badger's sett and a fox's hole and were taken to a bank where there was a positive warren of rabbits, although we did not see the rabbits themselves, only their droppings — and these were much mixed up with those of sheep,' said Isobel. 'No doubt it was all very interesting for those who like that kind of thing, but all it reminded me of was the dreary nature walks we used to take under the guidance of our botany lecturer at college. Anyway, my feet are killing me. Chuck me the *Sunday Express*. I can usually do their general knowledge crossword if it doesn't include the names of politicians or anything to do with electricity.'

'You filled in *ohm* last Sunday,' said Tamsin.

'No. It filled itself in from the "down" columns, so that saw me through. I would scorn to know anything about a subject which all our sixth-form boys have at their fingertips.'

After lunch she announced her intention of spending the afternoon with the newspaper and with her feet up. Hermione, who had taken her long walk before breakfast as well as the later one with the forester, was also disinclined for further exertion.

At half-past two, just as the washing-up was finished, John Trent came over and offered to take Tamsin and Erica in his car to make, as far as possible, the same round as the other two had done that morning with the forester.

'We had a reclining seat put in the car for my mother,' he said, looking at Tamsin, 'so I can put it back for you to keep your foot up. My parents always snooze on Sunday afternoons, so I'd be pleased to have something to do.'

Tamsin reported that her ankle was so much easier that she had no need to keep her foot up, but would be glad to go out in a car and follow the forest trails so far as this was possible.

'I think I've walked most of them,' said John. 'Of course,

walking is the only real way to get to know a countryside.'

'A sage remark,' said Isobel, 'but Hermione and I defaulted this morning. We dodged the column at the second viewpoint after we'd seen a farm and some sheep. My legs were giving way beneath me and my mind was giving way under a mass of information. I spend my working life dishing out information to others, but I find it difficult to digest when it's dished out to me.'

'I shall try not to bore the passengers. If they prefer it, I will do nothing except answer questions.'

'And will you stop the car if I ask you?' said Tamsin.

'Yes, of course. Do you get car-sick?'

'Oh, heavens, no! I'm a painter and I shall be on the lookout for anything that seems to be in my line because this is a working holiday for me.'

'I say! Have you had anything hung?'

'Only a hare somebody sent her last year,' said Isobel, 'and after she'd hung it according to instructions, she liked the look of what was happening to it so little that she asked the man next door to bury it. He didn't, of course. He ate it and said he enjoyed it very much.'

'It nearly turned her into a vegetarian,' said Erica, 'or so she told me in a letter. This holiday is a get-together for the three of us. We're all working-girls and don't see a great deal of one another as a general rule.'

John picked up Tamsin, when he had brought his car round to the foot of the cabin steps, and installed her in the front seat, where there was more leg-room than Erica had at the back. They were out until five and Tamsin was lyrical when they returned and John had gone.

'We've been out on to the moors as well as in the forest,' she said, 'and there are lots of bits I want to paint. We were able to leave the car on the edge of the woods and John wouldn't let me do any real walking, but with his help —'

'The strong man carried her,' said Erica. 'Why do I weigh ten and a half stone and look like a baby elephant, while she looks like a wistful wraith and is all pale and interesting with a wrenched ankle?'

'There was something in the woods which he very much wanted us to see,' said Tamsin.

'One of these awful warnings,' said Erica, 'that we must point out to you two when we get the chance. Deadly poisonous, my dears, and easily mistaken by the uninitiated for a true, wholesome, delicious mushroom. It even grows in the same places as mushrooms. It's called the Death-Cap and you don't know you've been poisoned until twelve hours after you've eaten it and then it's usually too late for any antidote to work.'

'So the great thing,' said Tamsin, 'is to distinguish it from the harmless mushroom and avoid it. It grows in deciduous woods in the autumn and on all kinds of soil and its Latin name is *Amanita phalloides*. It can have a yellowish or greenish or brownish cap and it even has one of those sort of frills round its neck like a true mushroom. John says fatalities from eating it are more common on the Continent than over here because foreigners are more adventurous with their fungi than we are, but he thought he ought to warn us about the Death-Cap all the same.'

'Rather like it and just as poisonous, he says, is the Destroying Angel, *Amanita virosa*, but fortunately it's rare in this country and he couldn't find a specimen to show us,' said Erica. 'What is it that seems so thrilling about poisons?'

'We had all this information from our forester,' said Isobel. 'In answer to your question, I suppose it's simply the possibility of causing death which provides the titillation. You can't be bothered with a crime novel which doesn't have at least one murder in it, can you? That's why poisoning is interesting. It's so often deliberate, you see, and so desperately wicked, at that — worse, I mean, than bashing somebody over the head or even strangling them — that it has the fascination which makes evil so much more interesting than goodness. Look at schools. It's the rule-breakers, the pests, the sinners, who get all the attention and most of the limelight, not the decent, middle-of-the-road, non-teacher-baiting herd which, fortunately for us poor pedagogues, still forms the main body of the population.'

Erica returned to the original subject.

'Anyway, I'm glad I know about *Amanita phalloides*,' she

said, 'because it really does look so much like mushroom that you could easily mistake it if you hadn't been warned.'

'I don't know why you two were bored this morning,' said Tamsin, 'It wasn't only the fungi. We've had a wonderful time. John took us all over the place. Wherever the car could go, we went. There's nothing he doesn't know. We even had the good luck to see a fox.'

'You live in the country, Hermione. Have you any views on fox-hunting?' asked Erica.

'Not really. I don't think ours is hunting country. Bicester would be the nearest. I don't care enough either way to get hot under the collar. I once walked a hound puppy and thought it was perfectly charming and a friend of mine brought up a fox-cub which she adored, so what's the answer?'

'That only man is vile,' said Isobel, 'but we knew that, anyway.'

'Telephone!' said Laura Gavin, getting up from the table. 'Must be a wrong number. Who would telephone us at this time of day?'

'Finish your dinner,' said Dame Beatrice Lestrange Bradley. 'I will answer it.' She went out of the room and presently found herself in conversation with Hermione's mother.

'I'm a bit puzzled,' said Mrs Jenny Lestrange. 'You know that Hermione was going to spend a fortnight with my sister Sarah? Well, there is mumps in the house, so they can't have her. Instead of coming straight home she seems to have fixed up to stay with some people with whom she spent last night. She picked them up on the moors. I suppose it's all right? Young people do these casual things nowadays, don't they?'

'Picked them up on the moors?' said Dame Beatrice. 'That sounds odd and intriguing. However, I think the fact that the pronoun in the accusative case is in the plural should reassure you. Had she said she had picked *him* up on the moors, you might have cause for speculation. I take it that you are slightly perturbed, or you would not have telephoned.'

'She phoned me just a few minutes ago to say she has been invited to stay at this shack in the forest at a place called Wayland.

She thought at first that it was only for one night, but now it seems just possible that she may put in a fortnight with these people at their express invitation.'

'Well, Hermione is a sensible girl. I do not suppose there is anything to worry about.'

'I'm not exactly *worried*. The thing is that I can't get in touch with her over the telephone unless she rings me first. There is only a public call-box where she is. I have written to her to ask her to keep in contact with us, but no post goes out from here until tomorrow morning and goodness knows whether letters ever get to this wooden hut of hers, anyway.'

'Wayland? A wooden hut? Oh, it will be on Forestry Commission property, and perfectly respectable. It is a holiday centre.'

'What, at this time of year?'

'Mellow autumn, "close bosom-friend of the maturing sun." Autumn is a worthy season for holidays and immortal verse.'

'Keats was thinking about September, not October. He says the swallows were gathering; that means they hadn't migrated. I wish the starlings would migrate instead of being joined by hordes of their relations who *do* migrate from further north, and sometimes I think the whole lot of them descend on this farm. They even chivvy the cats if I put food out, and one really doesn't want the stable cats indoors. Look, Aunt dear, I'd go myself if Hermione didn't get so resentful when she thinks I'm coming the old hen over her young life, but I really would like to know what's going on in this holiday place.'

'Very well. I'll get Laura to call on her if that will ease your mind.'

'Well, it all sounds so bizarre. *Why* should she pick these women up on the moor? It's so Wuthering Heights of her! Will you really send Laura? I would be rather relieved. Hermione certainly won't resent *her*, and I don't want to seem to be making a fuss.'

'The excursion will combine very nicely with another assignment which Laura has in prospect. She is going to spend a week with her brother in Scotland. She can call on Hermione, stay the night at the hotel in York which she has already booked — it means going back on her tracks a bit, but she won't mind that — and from York she will telephone me and I will pass her report on to you.'

Laura, apprised of the commission, expressed pleasure. She and Dame Beatrice breakfasted early so that Laura could start in good time, and by half-past eight she was on her way northwards. Maps had located the village of Wayland and an enquiry at the post office there, when she reached it, took her to the two-mile drive which led to the reception centre and the warden's office. Here she was directed to the cabin, for Hermione had mentioned Erica's name in her telephone message to her mother and Jenny had passed it on to Dame Beatrice. When Laura found the cabin it was half-past five and all the occupants were at home, for Erica and Tamsin had returned from their excursion with John Trent while Hermione and Isobel, content with their morning walk under the guidance of the forester, had remained in the cabin as they had planned to do.

Erica answered Laura's knock on the door, but as soon as she heard Laura's voice Hermione flew out to the vestibule.

'You're in time for tea, ' she said, when she had embraced her. 'What on earth are you doing in these parts?'

'Thank goodness for a cuppa. I am on my way to Scotland. Dame B. is at home. Your mother told us you were here, so, as it was more or less on my way, I thought I would look you up.'

Introductions were made, Laura had tea with the party and later from her hotel made her report over the telephone to Dame Beatrice.

'I've had a good journey. Located the log hut. Very civilised and all mod con, tell Jenny. Hermione came to the rescue on the moors because one of the girls had sprained her ankle. There are three of them. One is a teacher, the sprained ankle is a painter of Christmas and birthday cards and pet animals, the oldest one is an accounts clerk to a builder who happens to be her father, and the whole set-up could not be more innocuous and respectable. All they are going to do is drive about the neighbourhood looking at the scenery and visiting places of interest and "unspoiled natural beauty", as the conservationists put it. They propose also to breathe the fresh (and it *is* fresh!) moorland air and follow well-trodden tracks through the woods noting the fauna and flora.'

'I wonder whether a fortnight of such idyllic existence will be too much for Hermione,' said Dame Beatrice. 'Will the others make interesting companions?'

'I think so. Two of the women are in their thirties. One is sardonic and quite bracing, the other (the builder's daughter) very motherly and kind, and the painter is about Hermione's age and a bit of a sensitive plant, apart from her ankle, but they seem quite a good lot and very pleasant. So far there don't seem to be any men involved, although the young one and the motherly one did go out in a neighbour's car this afternoon to learn the local geography and (I gather) to be given a botany lesson on trees, plants and toadstools from a young fellow who seems knowledgeable in such matters. Anyway, Hermione is in good hands and the woods are glorious. I could wish I were staying in the cabin myself, except that we have the New Forest on our own doorstep. Reassure Jenny. There is nothing to worry about — and those are *not* famous last words. I hope not, anyway.'

# −3−

# LOUSEWORT

'I'm getting restless and peevish,' said Tamsin after lunch next day. 'It's lovely weather and I want to go out and find something to paint. I can't walk much because of this damned ankle, but if one of you would take me out on to the moors, I'm sure I could hirple my way well enough to get down to that beck I saw yesterday when Erica and I were out with John.'

'So long as you go easy you'll be all right,' said Erica. 'That strapping I've put on should hold the ankle. Isobel wants to see Long Cove Bay, so I'll take her in my car if Hermione doesn't mind taking you in hers.'

Hermione brought her car round and was relieved to note that Tamsin required very little assistance to get down the steps and cross the five yards of rough grass to the car. In no time they were passing the warden's office and were out on the trail Hermione had followed with the forester and Tamsin with John Trent.

They came out by the Wayland signpost and were soon crossing the moor in the long slant which Hermione had seen ahead of her when she had realised she was lost. That Saturday evening seemed now to be a very long way behind her.

'There should be a track over to the left just before we get to a bridge,' said Tamsin. 'We could turn off there, perhaps. I'm sure there ought to be something good. I want a dip in the moor with the beck going through it.'

'Right. I'll go slowly. Tell me when to stop and then I'll do a scramble and come back and tell you what's down in the dip. No point in putting that foot to the ground any more often than you need.'

The little stone bridge came into sight and the moorland track which Tamsin remembered from the day before ran out into a limitless expanse of heather. It was narrow and bumpy and Hermione drove slowly. It led suddenly and steeply downhill and then wound away upwards across a shoulder of the moor before it dipped down again to the beck.

Tamsin called a halt and said that, if Hermione was prepared to explore, this was a likely spot.

Hermione pulled up. A tiny path went off to the right and before she got very far she could hear the splashing sound of the beck. Soon she could see it not very far below her. It was bubbling over flat boulders and smaller stones and on the further side of it was a low hill with a rounded summit. The foot of the hill was strewn with more boulders and a rough path of varying width ran beside the stream and led on the right to a more distant and higher hill. A narrow stone bridge without copings, possibly a pack-horse bridge, lay across the stream and there was another and a rougher path on the other side of the water.

Hermione picked out the flattest bit of the path on her own side and went back to the car for the camp stool and folding chair they had put in the boot.

'You don't seem to have brought paints and things,' she said on her return, when she had set up the stool and chair.

'No, I don't need them. I'm only going to make a sketch and a note of the colours. It's enough for my kind of work. I can do the painting sitting on the balcony of the cabin.'

With Hermione's help she managed the downward slope without too much difficulty and settled herself to her sketching. Hermione sat down and took out her cigarettes. She watched the artist at work for a bit and then said,

'If you don't mind, I'd like to do a bit of exploring. You'll be all right, won't you?'

'Oh, yes. I've got the view I want. I shall need about half an hour.'

'Good. I shan't be long.' She followed the path on her side of the beck and was soon mounting steadily. The path twisted and serpentined through dead bracken, grew rougher and then narrower. She stopped and looked back once or twice. Sometimes she could get a sight of Tamsin, sometimes the artist was hidden from view when the path took one of its sharp bends. The hillside was strewn with limestone boulders which looked like grey-fleeced wethers among the brown bracken. As she mounted she could see further hills.

She was gone for much longer than she had intended. When she returned by the same route — there was no other — it was to find that Tamsin had company, an eventuality she had not bargained for. Standing behind Tamsin and watching her at work was a sturdily-built man, hardly more than a youth, dressed in shorts, a leather jacket and heavy shoes. He had a rucksack on his shoulders and was wearing a rather rakish Tyrolean hat with a little red feather in it.

Hermione walked up to him.

'Have you my friend's permission to stand here and look over her shoulder?' she asked.

'It's all right,' said Tamsin without looking up. 'He isn't bothering me and I've nearly finished all I can do here.'

'I could show her some better bits than this,' said the youth. 'I live around here and I know the moors pretty well. What would you say to a farm?'

'A moorland farm?' asked Tamsin.

'Yes. That is to say, the farm itself is in a valley with pasture for sheep, but the moors rise right behind it, and it's a really beautiful setting for a picture.'

'How far is it?' asked Hermione.

'A dozen miles or so, the way I shall show you. There are one or two bits an artist might like to see on the way. Have you come far?'

'No. We've got a holiday cabin in the Forestry Commission's woods,' replied Tamsin.

'Oh, that's all right, then. When you've seen the farm, I can show you a short cut home. All main road, once you come up out of the valley. All you have to do is to look out for a signpost to Gledge End. You can easily find your way from there. By the way, my name is Adam Penshaw.'

'Tamsin Lindsay and this is Hermione Lestrange.'

A dozen miles across the moor they came to a village. It was stone-built and almost hidden away among tall trees in their autumn colouring. It had a small, squat-towered church and out beyond it, where the road rose again, was a lonely public house with a thatched entrance-porch and two of its four upstairs windows bricked up.

'Shouldn't think they get much custom there,' said Hermione, as they passed it and the car took a winding, uphill road back on to the moor. 'It's very much isolated.'

'Oh, it's not all that far from the village,' said the youth. 'It used to be the shepherds' pub when there were more sheep about than there are now.'

'I think it would make a picture,' said Tamsin. 'One day we must have a drink there.'

The road still rose and around it, in front and on both sides, was the emptiness of the moor. On they went, up and over the hill, and Hermione was about to ask how much further they had to go when the countryside began to change. As they dipped down into the valley, the moor still rose away to the right, but there were some trees on grassy hillocks and when they reached a farm there were sheep and one or two cows grazing the sloping pastures.

The farm buildings were few. There was the farmhouse itself, red-roofed and with three chimneys. A small barn was behind it and almost adjoining the house on the side furthest from the travellers was a cattle-shed with some of the roof-tiles missing and with the farmyard midden in front of it.

Hermione stopped the car and Adam leaned forward from the back seat and asked, 'Well, what about it, Tamsin? Do you want to get out and make a sketch?'

'Not now,' she said, 'but perhaps another time.'

'Look here, how much further are you taking us?' asked Hermione. 'I'm not a bit keen on driving over moorland roads after dark.'

'Oh, you've seen nothing yet. Just press on a bit.'

They left the farm behind and the road mounted to the moors again. Hermione began to feel more and more dubious about the route they were taking and when the road made a hairpin bend she was moved to expostulate.

'Oh, look here!' she said. 'You told us it was about twelve miles. We must have done twice that already.'

'Ah, but you haven't seen the view I wanted Tamsin to get. We're almost at the junction with the main road to Gledge End. Pull up here and take a look.'

Hermione drew up at the side of the road. As soon as she had done so, the youth picked up his rucksack, which he had unslung and placed beside him on the back seat, and hopped smartly out of the car.

'Thanks a lot for the lift,' he said. 'I'm staying just over there.' He indicated a large house about two hundred yards away to the left. 'Be seeing you.'

'I don't think he will!' said Hermione furiously. 'I've a good mind to get out and heave a rock at him. Of all the nerve! All he wanted was a lift home. Why couldn't he have said so, instead of leading us this dance? Now what do we do?'

'Keep straight on and hope he was telling us the truth about the main Gledge End road,' said Tamsin.

'We must be nearly at the coast!'

This proved to be the case, and when they reached the town which was signposted Long Cove Bay, there was the turning to Gledge End which the youth had promised.

'I don't altogether blame him,' said Tamsin, waiting to make the remark until she deduced that Hermione had simmered down. 'I suppose he'd have had to sleep in the heather if he hadn't met us, and it's not the best time of year to do that.'

Hermione snorted and made no attempt at any other reply. All the same, the main road, making some magnificent sweeps around the higher parts of the moor, was broad and well-surfaced and she realised that there was no need to go into Gledge End, for she found a narrow turning to Wayland and it was not quite dark by the time they stopped the car outside the cabin and the other two had come out to help Tamsin up the steps.

'You're later than we expected,' said Erica. 'We almost thought of sending out a search-party.'

'We fell among thieves,' said Tamsin. 'Well, there was one thief, anyway. He stole our time and our petrol. Wait until Hermione gets back from the carpark and then we'll tell you all about it.'

'You ought to have come with us to Long Cove Bay. It's a delightful fishing-village built in steps and slopes and all queer little corners and nooks and crannies. You'd love it. There must be lots of bits you'd like to sketch.'

'Thanks. I think we've been to it, near enough. I wouldn't mind going there again, but Hermy One is livid about this wretched youth who hi-jacked us into giving him a lift, so I don't think I'll suggest it at present.'

Hermione returned from the carpark with her equanimity restored. She had encountered John Trent, told him the story and they had laughed about it. She had mentioned the large house for which the youth had been making after he had jumped out of the car and she had described the rest of the locality and the turning on to the main road to Gledge End.

'John says the house is a Youth Hostel,' she concluded, 'and the beastly boy would never have made it if we hadn't picked him up, so I suppose we did our good deed for the day, however inadvertently. Oh, and John says that it's worthwhile to take a look at the big notice-board in the reception centre from time to time, especially if the weather turns wet, because there is often some sort of entertainment laid on for the cabin people.'

'Well, I expect it would only be a sing-song or the local pop group,' said Isobel, 'but it might make a change from sitting indoors and listening to the rain on the roof.'

There was no rain on the following day and plans had just been made for a whole day out, with a pub lunch, when there came a knock at the door. Erica, as usual, was the one to answer it. She came back to say that a boy wanted to know whether he could guide Tamsin to any more beauty spots.

'I suppose he's the boy you picked up yesterday,' she added.

'Do you want to speak to him?'

'No, we don't,' said Hermione, 'except to thank him kindly and tell him to clear off.'

'Sorry,' said Erica, returning to the door, 'but all our plans are made. Did they take you in at the Youth Hostel?'

'Oh, yes. I'd booked, but I got out of the coach at Gledge End when I ought to have stayed in for Long Cove Bay, so it was a real bonus meeting your friends.'

'Yes, but not for them. Well, thanks for calling, but please don't bother any more.'

'I've hired a motorbike, so any messages you want run, shopping, errands —'

'No, thank you. We can manage perfectly well for ourselves.'

'I wonder how he found out where we were staying?' said Tamsin, when the door was shut.

'You as good as told him, I expect,' said her sister.

'But there are over thirty of these cabins. He can hardly have tried every one until he found ours.'

'I suppose you told him your name. He had only to go to the office and say he had a message for you. Erica booked the cabin, but all our names are in the warden's book. You can't stay anywhere *incognito* unless you're a member of the criminal classes.'

'Oh, well, we've given him the bird,' said Erica comfortably. 'I expect he was surprised to meet me on the doorstep. He probably thought Tamsin and Hermy were here on their own. Ask me and I'd say he's a poisonous little reptile. You get to spot them when you have to employ a certain amount of casual labour, as we have to do on our building sites when the pressure of work is heavy. Well, which car are we going to use? No sense in taking both as we're going to stick together today.'

It was Tamsin who had mapped out the route. As none of the others minded where they went, she had selected two subjects for her sketches. One of these involved a seascape, so, after a midday snack at a pub in a seaside town about thirty miles from the forest, she and Hermione boarded a pleasure steamer which made the coastal trip to a famous headland while the two older women explored the town.

Hermione was studying the coast through binoculars when Tamsin said, 'Stand by! Here's that boy Adam again.'

However, he did not attempt to come up and speak to them and it was with a slight sense of triumph that they reported this to the other two whom they met again on the quay.

'He's accepted the brush-off, then,' said Erica. 'Good for him.'

'A bit of a coincidence, though, his choosing to come to this place on the day we've chosen to come here, and to catch the boat those two were on. The trips run every hour, weather permitting, and today the weather does permit, although it must be very near the end of the season,' said Isobel. 'I think the wretched youth was trailing us.'

'Oh, forget him!' said Hermione. The next stop was at an ancient abbey on the further side of Gledge End. Tamsin, who had seen photographs, wanted to sketch the view of the ruins which was to be obtained through the great rounded arch of the gatehouse. They found the place without difficulty and she remained in the front seat of the car to make her drawing through the glass of the windscreen while the other three explored the ruins.

She sketched in the archway. It was complete in itself although the walls in which it had been set were in ruins, and she was making rapid, expert strokes to indicate the broken arc where a rose window of the abbey church had been partly demolished to leave only a finger of masonry pointing to the sky, when she was interrupted. The driver's door was pulled open and Adam Penshaw inserted himself into the driver's seat.

'Carry on! Carry on! Don't mind me,' he said. Startled — for she had been too much absorbed in her work to hear him come up, Tamsin dropped her pencil. As he bent to pick it up she snatched out the car-key which was opposite him and dropped it into her jacket pocket.

He knew what she had done. He laughed as he handed back the pencil.

'Did you think I was going to run off with you?' he asked. Tamsin made a few quick strokes to her sketch of the sky-pointing finger of church masonry before she answered him.

'No, of course not,' she said, 'but I never trust an adolescent sense of humour.'

'Oh, come, now! Don't you like me?'

'It is not a question of liking or not liking. I don't want to seem unkind, but look here, now. My sister and I see all too little of one another when her school terms begin. We don't live together, you see, because I still live at home, whereas she has to live reasonably near her school. She has always been friendly with Erica, but, there again, they see all too little of one another because their homes are so far apart. Can't you understand that a small group of women sometimes want and even *need* to be on their own and to enjoy female companionship and a single-sex natter now and again?'

'What about Hermione?' he asked, ignoring her plea. 'Where does she come in?'

'She is a bird of passage. She rescued the perishing when I hurt my ankle and she rescued *you*. We are very glad to have her with us, but I warn you that she doesn't want a young boy horning in on our holiday any more than *we* do.'

'I'm *not* a young boy, dammit!'

'All right, then, be a grown-up gentleman and get out of the car. Just leave us alone. Forget us, there's a nice person.' She spotted Erica, who was crossing the front of the ruins. 'The others are coming back,' she said. He took the hint and skipped out of the car. This time she heard the engine of his motorcycle (a sound which must have gone unnoticed by her when he had arrived) and he careered off.

'He seems to have taken a fancy to you,' said Erica, when she had come back to the car and had been told of Adam's invasion of it. 'It looks as though one of us had better stay with you in future. What a nuisance the wretched boy is! Oh, well, let's hope you've really choked him off this time.'

Such was not the case, but Adam made only one more attempt to seek their society. This happened on the same evening. They were late enough home from their excursion to decide to combine tea and supper and then to sit about until ten or when they felt ready for bed.

The weather was changing by the time the meal was over; by eight o'clock the wind had got up and before nine the rain was lashing the windows. Woodwork in the cabin creaked and moaned and occasionally let off a sharp, protesting crack.

'You'd think it is still alive,' said Tamsin.

'What is?' asked Hermione.

'The wood this place is made of. You know, there's something creepy about a forest in this sort of weather. It's as though the living trees were calling out to the dead ones.'

'Oh, go to bed and pull the coverlet over your ears!' said Isobel. 'That's what I'm going to do.' The wind gave a sudden howl and there was a crash as a particularly rough squall hit the french doors. ' "It's the wild night outside". That's from *Campbell of Kilmhor*, my favourite one-act play.'

' "Is the rain still coming down?" ' quoted Tamsin in her turn.

' "It is that, then". What's the bit about some poor lost soul coming up to the door, and we refusing it shelter?'

'Oh, you two!' said Erica. 'Shut up! You make me go all goose-flesh. Let's do the washing-up.'

'Can't it stay till morning?' asked Isobel.

'No, it jolly well can't. If I begin to let you lot slack off, this place will be a pigsty by Saturday.'

Adam's last visit to them was heralded by a furious battering on the french doors, a sound which outdid even the fury of the storm.

'Oh, Lord! What now?' said Erica, who had been the last to get into bed when the washing-up was done.

'It's only the wind,' said Tamsin.

'It certainly isn't.' The almost frenzied banging came again. Erica rolled out of bed, pulled on her dressing-gown and went into the lounge. 'Who is it?' she called out.

'Let me in! My bike's conked out and I'm soaked to the skin. Open the door!'

'I can't. We're all in bed!'

'Let me in, I tell you! I'm nearly drowned!' The hammering came again, a positive fusillade. This time it had an effect, but not the one which Adam intended. Another voice, deeper than his own, said, 'What's all this?'

'Oh, John! John Trent!' shouted Erica. There was a yell and an indeterminate scrabbling noise. Then John Trent called out, 'All right, ladies! All clear now!' Erica opened the door. John Trent, torch in hand, was on the verandah. Erica pulled him inside.

'Oh, dear! You *are* wet!' she said.

'Nothing to speak of. What was all that racket?'

'That was the wretched boy who's been dogging our footsteps for the past two days. We thought we'd got rid of him.'

'You don't value him, then?'

'We're sick to death of him.'

'Oh, that's all right, then. I've just chucked him over your verandah railings.'

'Oh, dear!' said Tamsin, distressed.

'Don't worry. I'll retrieve him and bed him down in our shack. He can have the spare bunk and I'll chase him away in the morning with a flea in his ear that he won't forget. I'm sorry he's made such a nuisance of himself. I'll see it doesn't happen again.'

# — 4 —

# DODDER

After breakfast on the following day Erica paid a visit to the cabin across the way to thank John Trent for his intervention.

'But for you, it looks as though we might have been pestered by that youth for the rest of our stay,' she said.

'Oh, no, I don't think so. If he is staying at Youth Hostels he is allowed a maximum of three nights in any one of them. It was abominable of him to attempt to knock you up at that time of night, but I don't think you'll see or hear any more of him. I've put his motorcycle right and sent him off.'

She had scarcely got back to her own cabin when she and the others had another visitor. This was the warden. He was accompanied by the forester who had led the conducted tour on the Sunday.

'Not to alarm you,' he said, 'but I'm making a round of the cabins because I have just had a police message. A convict has escaped from Hangmoor. He will be in need of money and a change of clothes. The police don't think he has any outside contacts. He's a convicted murderer, not a habitual criminal, but he must be desperate and may be dangerous. The police think he is somewhere on the moors and will soon be recaptured, but until that happens it might be as well to stick to the forest walks, or, if you do go out on the moors, to remain in your car and on no account to give anybody a lift. Anyway, whatever you do or wherever you go, my advice is that you all keep together and make sure that your cabin is locked up when you're out and is made secure at night.'

John Trent came over after the warden had gone.

'My parents and I are checking out on Saturday morning,' he said, 'and I don't know whether our cabin has been booked for the following week. If it should be left empty you'll be rather isolated out here, so you'll be a bit careful until this fellow is caught, won't you?'

'You know, said Tamsin, when John had left them, 'I think all that business with Adam has upset my nervous system. I don't believe I want to go out today.'

'That's nonsense,' said Isobel. 'We mustn't give in to a scare. There isn't one chance in a thousand that we shall run across this murderer. As for Adam Penshaw, well, he was just a nuisance to you, and that was your own fault. You shouldn't have encouraged him in the first place.'

'I suppose I encouraged him too, you know,' said Hermione. 'I gave him the lift in my car. Who was to know that he would latch on to us the way he did?'

'Well, the rain has stopped,' said Erica, 'and I can't see us spending all our time cooped up indoors just because there's a convict on the run. Why don't we try one of the forest trails if Tamsin's ankle will stand up to a bit of walking? We need not go all that far.'

'Oh, the ankle is all right. I'll buy an ash-plant just in case. I expect they've got some at the shop,' said Tamsin. 'If not, they'll have them in Gledge End.'

'We'll each buy one,' said Hermione, 'and then it won't matter how many escaped convicts we meet.'

'We're not likely to meet any in the forest,' said Isobel, 'with the foresters and the other cabin people all over the place. I'm game for a walk. Who's coming?'

Into the outhouse at the Youth Hostel slunk a bedraggled, dirty, unshaven man. The outhouse was an open-fronted shed with a bench on all three sides. It was there to accommodate Youth

Hostellers who arrived before five in the afternoon, since the hostel admitted nobody before that hour. The man knew nothing of this. He was merely taking a much-needed rest. When he heard voices he got up from the bench and almost collided with two young men who were about to enter the outhouse.

'No good trying yet. It wants a quarter to five,' said one. 'I say! You're wet, brother! Been sleeping rough?'

'Lost my way,' said the man, trying to push past.

'Mean you were out in the rain last night? They've got a drying-room here. You'll be all right by morning.'

'Drying room?'

'Sure. Dry your gear, see? Haven't you stayed in one of these before?'

'One of what?'

'Aren't you a member?'

'Member of what? I've got to get on. Let me by.'

'Where are you bound for?'

'What's that to you?' He pushed past and plunged downhill on to the moor, but the questioner was not to be put off so easily. He ran after him and caught up with him. The man turned on him like an angry cat. 'Let me be! Get lost!' he said hoarsely.

'I can't let you be, brother. You'd be on my conscience. Look, you're down on your luck. I can see that. Come back with me to the hostel and I'll get you a bed. A mate of mine can't come and I've got his membership ticket as well as my own. You can be him, so far as the hostel will know. The Lord will forgive me the bit of cheating, as it's in a good cause. Come on back with me. I'll see you through. Got any money?'

'What do *you think?*'

'I don't think you have, but the bed is paid for. We have to book and pay in advance. On the road, are you?' All this time the earnest young man had remained with a sinewy hand grasping the wanderer's sleeve. The unkempt man ceased to resist. 'Would they really give me a bed?' he asked.

'Sure, if I show them the card. Your name's Bert Leeds for tonight. Got it? Bert Leeds. That's who you are, and you have to leave before ten in the morning. Now I don't ask any questions, so

you don't need to tell me any lies. I want to be your friend,
brother, that's all. You see, I believe we were put into this sinful
world to help each other, so I'm going to help you. Just between
ourselves, what's your name? I want to pray for you.'

'I don't have a name and prayers won't do me any good.'

'Oh, well, brother, if that's the way you want it, I won't press
you. Where are you making for?'

'I've got to get to Gledge End, so let me get on.'

'You'll never make it across the moor tonight. You look to me
like you've got a weak chest. You come on back with me, brother.
I'm not going to have your death on my conscience.'

'What did you say my name was?'

'Bert Leeds. All I have to do is hand in the cards and collect
them up again when we leave.'

'I'll have to leave early.'

'That's all right. You leave as early as you like.' The other
young man came up to them. 'Oh, hullo, Tony,' said the Good
Samaritan. 'Are they open?'

'They are, Steve, they are.'

The bedraggled man licked his lips.

'I haven't heard those blessed words since I don't know when,'
he said. The young men laughed.

'Not that kind of open, brother,' said his rescuer. 'We're
strictly T.T. Come on, and I'll stake you to a tin of beans.'

The four young women found that the walk through the woods
was not an unqualified success. It was extremely wet underfoot
after the rain, the trees dripped relentlessly on to the walkers who
had a tendency to keep glancing from side to side in a wary, in fact
nervous, manner, and at the end of a mile Tamsin's ankle was
beginning to feel the strain of coping with slippery mud and the
heaps of sodden, fallen leaves.

With the help of Erica's walking-stick as well as her own, she
managed to get back to the carpark and the reception room,
where Erica commanded her to sit and rest while she herself
brought the car across the clearing.

'I was looking at the notice-board while you were gone,' said

Isobel, when they had got themselves and Tamsin into the car. 'There are some folk-dancers coming to give a show in a church hall at Gledge End on Saturday afternoon. The warden here has tickets. Shall we go?'

'How much are the tickets?' asked Erica.

'Fifty pence and downwards, Mistress Shylock.'

'For that dirty crack I shall treat you all, so there!'

The Youth Hostel was a popular one, but, so late in the holiday season, it was not full. Steve handed in the three tickets and he and Tony were soon making use of one of the calor gas cookers to heat up baked beans and fry the sausages they had bought at the hostel shop. Their guest ate his share, but remained taciturn. He did, however, insist upon doing the washing-up unassisted. After that, he asked where his bed was, so Steve showed him a large dormitory crowded with bunk beds, and he said he would turn in. The other two went into Long Cove Bay, the fishing village near by, to take a look at the sea, but by nine o'clock they, too, were in their bunks, and the hostel locked its doors at ten.

The warden did not live on the premises, but had what had been the lodge when the big Victorian house had been a private residence. She came over at seven in the morning to hand out the after-breakfast chores of cleaning and tidying-up which the hostellers were pledged to carry out before they left and to hand back membership tickets to those who were checking-out.

There was no sign of their overnight guest when Steve and Tony turned out of their bunks at eight. Steve applied to the warden.

'Oh,' she said, 'I expect he's the energetic sort. He must have gone out before I came over. His name is Leeds, you say? Well, he certainly hasn't checked out because his membership card is still here.'

'He'll have to get his own breakfast, then, when he gets back,' said Tony. 'One thing, it's only tea and cereal and baps and that pot of marmalade we bought here at the shop last night.'

They prepared their own breakfast and ate without talking. At nine they had performed the tasks allotted them by the warden but they still hung on without, at first, sharing the thought which was in both their minds.

At a quarter to ten the warden said brightly, 'Well, you two are quite the last. You know I have to close the hostel at ten, don't you? I should think your friend has decided to go on ahead of you.'

'Well, we can't wait any longer for him,' said Steve. He collected the three tickets and he and Tony went out to the vestibule where all outdoor boots and shoes had to be left so that mud was not brought into the public rooms. 'He's cut his stick, I reckon,' he added to Tony when they were out of earshot of the warden.

He had not only left the hostel, they discovered. He had taken Steve's anorak and rucksack with him. Steve was too godly a young man to swear. Instead, his eyes filled with tears of self-pity and disappointment.

'And I helped him and I trusted him,' he said. 'I called him brother. I was a Good Samaritan unto him. Our iron rations of biscuits and chocolate were in that rucksack, as well as all my spares.'

He could say no more at the time, for the warden came out after them. She still spoke brightly.

'Oh, well, if you're off, I can lock up now,' she said. 'I hope you catch up with your friend, but I daresay he's on his way back here by now to join you unless he's run into the escaped convict.'

'Escaped convict?' said Tony.

'Why, yes. Didn't you see the notice I put in the common-room? It was for the benefit of the girls mostly. You boys can always take care of yourselves, can't you? Yes, I had a police warning. A convicted murderer has escaped from the Hangmoor gaol and is thought to be on the moors.'

The two young men looked at one another.

'Thanks for telling us,' said Tony. As they tramped down the lane towards the coast-road he said to Steve, 'What do you think? Was he? He could be, I suppose.'

'Whether he was or not, he's a dirty dodder,' said Steve morosely.

'You mean an artful dodger, old man.'

'No, I don't. I mean a dirty dodder.'

'What's a dodder?'

'It's a plant. My botany book says it's a vampire. It feeds solely on the sap of other plants, just as a vampire lives by sucking other people's blood. Besides, if this dodder of ours is a murderer, he must have sucked somebody's blood.'

'Oh, hang it all, you can't write him off like that. You only thought he was a tramp down on his luck, and I daresay that's all he was, you know.'

'I shall think twice another time. It's a bit hard if you only try to carry out your ideals and a serpent turns and bites you in the heel.'

'When we get to a telephone you'd better give a description of him to the police.

'How can I? They would ask all sort of questions and I should have to say I'd got him into the hostel on somebody else's ticket.'

'I don't suppose the police would worry about that. If he *is* the escaped murderer they ought to be told about him. You can describe your anorak and your rucksack, can't you? Lucky he didn't pinch your boots as well.'

'I don't suppose he could get them on. I've got small feet for my height. Why don't we flag down a likely car and hitch a lift? I don't feel like footslogging it all day. Somebody can jolly well do *me* a good turn for a change.'

'Where shall we go?' asked Erica, when they were all in the car after she had bought the tickets for the dancers' show.

'To identify this church hall and then south, more or less,' said Isobel.

'To keep out of the murderer's way?'

'We don't know which is his way. I said south because we haven't explored in that direction.'

Enquiry at the post office in Gledge End produced directions so that they found the church hall, and then Erica turned on to the outskirts of the southern end of the little town and took the road to Alderwood where there were castle ruins for Tamsin to sketch and the others to explore.

'Although we'd better take it in turn to be with her in the car,' said Erica, 'in case our bright lad has taken it into his head to follow us again on that damned motorbike. Not you, Hermy. It would take Isobel or me to wipe the floor with him. Not that I think he'll bother us again.'

They saw nothing of Adam and had forgotten all about the convict until they had the most grim of reminders. They had tea at the only café in the little town of Alderwood and then, as there was plenty of daylight left, Erica decided to make a long cast round to get back to the forest and the cabin.

The route was supposed to take them across country by secondary roads to Gledge End and so home, but proved shorter than Erica had thought, so, instead of picking up the main road at a village called Yieldrigg, she went north on another secondary road with the intention of half-circling the forest area before dropping south again.

Eventually this brought them on to the moor and Hermione soon realised that they were on the road she had taken by mistake on her first journey. There was no fear of getting lost this time, as the neighbourhood was now familiar ground. She was looking out of the side window of the back seat which she was sharing with Isobel when she spotted the bicycle. Tamsin, seated beside the driver, saw it at the same moment and said, 'Somebody seems to have had a nasty spill. There's a bike in the heather.'

Erica pulled up on the verge.

'No reason for anybody to have had an accident on a road like this,' she said, 'unless there was a car involved.' Isobel said that perhaps they had better take a look. 'You and me,' she said to Erica. 'You two can stay with the car.'

# –5–

# BLOODSTAINED BRACKET

Tamsin, made unusally nervous because of her damaged and now treacherous ankle, said, 'Do be careful! There are stories of girls being pulled from bikes. This may have happened here. That convict, you know. He may still be about and he may be desperate for money.'

As soon as the other two had left the car Hermione got out too, went round to the driver's seat and joined Tamsin.

'Cheer up,' she said. 'If the convict pops out on them from one of the dips they can make a dash for it and I can start up the car in no time. But don't worry. He'll be far enough away by now. Is that ankle being a nuisance?'

'Aches a bit. It makes me feel helpless.'

'Yes, we shouldn't have let you walk on it. Keep a lookout on your side and if they begin to run I'll start the engine.'

'They've picked up the bike.'

'Yes. The front wheel looks as though it's buckled.'

'They're walking away from us.' Both girls watched as the older ones, having moved further off, stood with their backs to the car and looked into one of the dips in the moor. Then Erica went forward, while Isobel remained looking downwards. They returned at a sober pace and Hermione relinquished the driver's seat, but Erica said, 'I'm all shook up. It's rather nasty. We've got to go to Gledge End and see the police. You drive.'

'Well, of course you weren't to know, miss,' said the Superintendent of Police, 'but it's a pity you picked up the bicycle. We may have to depend on the handlebars for an attacker's dabs. Still, no doubt we can manage. We'll have to eliminate yours. Which of you picked up the bicycle? Both of you handled it? Of course we shall destroy your prints as soon as we've done with them. You need not think they'll be on permanent record. Staying in one of the forest cabins are you? If I might have the number? Right. Just out for a drive, you say, when one of you spotted the bike. Just so. Thought, when you found the body, that there might have been a hit-and-run motorist? On a lonely moorland road it's quite possible that's just what happened. We can't be sure until we get a full report of the injuries. A nasty experience for you ladies, but I'm bound to say that you have acted in a very public-spirited manner in looking about you and then coming straight to us to report that you found the body.'

'I rather wish we hadn't found it,' said Erica when they were back in the cabin. 'Her head was an awful mess. I've seen some results of accidents on the building sites, but I've never seen anything like that. Whoever did it, motorist or whatever, must be in a desperate flap to have dragged the body off the road and tumbled it into that dip. You'd have thought he would have chucked the bike in after it, and I wish to goodness he had. Then none of us would have spotted it and stopped to investigate, and somebody else, later on, would be carrying the can instead of us.'

'I expect his only idea was to make his getaway before another motorist came along,' said Tamsin. 'You think it *was* a motorist and not the convict, then?'

'I don't want to think at all. Yes, I'll have another cup of tea, please. No, nothing to eat. I couldn't face it.'

'Was it very bad?' said Hermione to Isobel when their door was shut and they were in their bunks that night.

'I didn't go close, but Erica is pretty tough and she said it made her feel sick. I saw a lot of blood on the face and clothes, that's all.'

'You don't suppose the police think *we* bumped her, do you?'
'Good heavens, no. Why should they?'

'Well, they might, that's all.'

'They wouldn't be so fatheaded. If we'd done it we should hardly have gone haring off to the police station to report it, should we?'

'Well, of course we would. Any decent person would.'

'Yes, but any decent person wouldn't have hidden the body in that hole. The person who did that wasn't going to run straight to the police. Look, are you trying to tell me something? Don't forget I spend my life dealing with cagey adolescents, so speak up.'

'I'm not an adolescent and I'm not cagey, but there's something perhaps I ought to tell you before the police spot it. You remember that Erica was a bit shaken and made me drive the car after she had seen the body?'

'Yes, of course.'

'First to the police station and then here to unload Tamsin and you two before I put the car into the carpark?'

'Yes, I remember all that. What about it?'

'Well, on the way to the carpark I had a skid on some wet leaves and hit a tree. Oh, no real damage done, and I'm going to tell Erica that I'm afraid I've marked her paint, but it has suddenly come to me that the police might decide to take a look at the car.'

'And think their own thoughts when they spot the marks? I shouldn't worry. I'm quite sure the scratches made by a tree-trunk wouldn't in the least resemble the marks made by the impact of a girl on a bike. Besides, we'll all back you up. You know that. Anyway, I'm glad you thought of it and told me. It can't have been very serious, or you would have told the three of us when you got back from the carpark.'

'It was dark, so I don't know what the damage is. It can't be anything much, because I corrected the skid and really only skimmed the tree.'

'Tell Erica in the morning and we'll go down and take a look. Meanwhile, forget it and go to sleep.'

'What did you two tell them at the police station?'

'Only what we've already told you. The girl was dead. We didn't touch the body — that is to say, Erica didn't and I didn't go down into the dip. We picked up the bicycle to see what the damage was and got a bit of a rocket from the superintendent because we had probably messed up any fingerprints there might be on the handlebars.'

'That was unfair. You didn't know at that point that the girl was dead. Was it just an accident, do you think?'

'I have no idea. Anyway, whether she was knocked off her bike by a car or whether the convict had had a go at her, somebody had dragged her away from the roadside and tried to hide the body, that's for sure. What's more, whoever it was must have been in a bit of a flap, or he would have hidden the bike, too. It was a clear giveaway to leave it at the roadside where anybody passing would spot it.'

'I don't know so much. Leaving it at the roadside would look as though a car had hit it, so, as the convict wouldn't have had a car, that would tend to tell in his favour, wouldn't it?'

'Then why try to hide the body?'

'Oh, to make it look as though the car-driver had taken the girl to hospital, I suppose.'

In the far bedroom the subject of conversation was on the same lines. 'Do the police think the convict did it?' asked Tamsin.

'I couldn't say. The police are like the doctors. They never tell you what they're thinking if they can possibly help it.'

'The bicycle being damaged makes it look more like a car accident with a hit-and-run driver, wouldn't you say?'

'It doesn't matter what I say. It is what the police think that counts. Go to sleep. I need to be fresh and bright when I meet them in the morning.'

'The police?'

'Who else? Don't you realise there's a fair chance they'll decide I could have been the driver who killed that girl?'

'But you and Isobel went to them straight away and reported finding the body.'

'That doesn't prove it wasn't my car which killed her.'

That there was considerable substance in this remark was proved in the middle of the next morning. Apart from some necessary shopping which was done at the little shop near the warden's office, nobody felt inclined for an outing and, after what had been said the night before, nobody was surprised when a detective-inspector and a sergeant turned up, just after the mid-morning coffee and biscuits had been cleared away, and asked for an interview.

Erica, as usual, answered the door.

'Good morning, miss. Detective-Inspector Ribble and Sergeant Nene. May we come in?'

'Of course.'

'Thank you, miss. Just one or two points and then we would like you to accompany us to your carpark. You were the driver, I believe you told the superintendent, miss.'

'Yes, I was. Won't you sit down?'

'Thank you, miss. Would you repeat what you reported yesterday about the route you took?' Erica repeated the information she had supplied at the police station. 'So you did not pass through Gledge End on your return?'

'Only on our outward journey. We went there to locate the church hall where there is to be an entertainment for which we have tickets.'

'Then you went on to —' he looked at the sergeant, who turned to his notebook and read aloud.

'That's right,' said Erica, when he had finished.

'So you were almost home when you saw the bicycle. I suppose it was getting near dusk by that time?'

'Oh, no, there was plenty of daylight left.'

'So you hadn't switched on the car lights?'

'It wasn't necessary.'

'Well, not in your opinion, anyway. I would like you to accompany me to the carpark. You *were* the driver when the bicycle came into view?'

'Yes, I drove the whole time until after we found the body. I was shaken up and thought I'd better not drive after that.'

'I took over,' said Hermione, 'and there is something I ought to tell you before you inspect the car.'

'Oh, yes, miss? What would that be?'

'I scratched the paint, I think, when the car skidded.'

'Oh, it skidded, did it?'

'Yes, on some slippery fallen leaves. I corrected the skid, but I think in doing so I slightly bumped a tree.'

'You — or somebody else — certainly bumped something, miss. We have already looked at the car.'

'In that case,' said Erica, 'why do you want *me* to look at it?'

'The car is marked, miss. Whether by a tree or a bicycle we don't yet know.'

'Oh, look here!' said Isobel. 'Our car never *touched* that bicycle!'

Erica returned from the carpark unaccompanied by the police, but she was looking worried.

'The car is marked all right,' she said. 'They don't exactly say they don't believe me, and it was good of you, Hermy, to speak up the way you did, but I'm afraid I'm for it. That policeman has got it all worked out, I think. He believes we ran down that girl and realised what we'd done — I mean that we'd killed her. He thinks we panicked and tried to hide the body and then thought again and decided to report it. He also thinks we concocted that story Hermy told about the skid just to account for the marks on the car.'

'Oh, dear, what a mess!' wailed Tamsin.

'But, look,' said Isobel, 'if the tree made marks on the car, the car must have made marks on the tree. Hermy, you probably know more or less whereabouts you were when you had the skid. The road ought to show some signs of it, and then all we have to do is to find the tree. Besides, surely their forensic experts, or whoever delves into these police things, can spot the difference between marks made by hitting a bike and marks made by bashing into a tree.'

'I didn't bash into it. I only sort of skimmed it. There might not be any recognisable marks on the tree at all.'

'But if the car is marked?' said Tamsin.

'That's the worst of this cheap paint they put on cars nowadays,' said Isobel. 'Come on, Hermy. Let's go and see if we can spot this tree of yours. Mind you watch your step! There may be a copper behind every bush keeping a suspicious eye on us.'

'I'll tell you what else I'm going to do,' said Hermione, when they were outside the cabin. 'Do you know what I think? I think the police have some reason for not suspecting that convict.'

'Picked him up before the girl was killed?'

'It's more than likely.'

'I hadn't thought of that. If that's so, then we, and especially poor old Erica, really *are* in the cart. So what's your idea?'

'To go straight to the telephone before we begin looking for trees and skidmarks and call up my great-aunt, only hoping she is free and at home. She will get us out of this mess if anybody can and a good old mess I think it's going to be.'

'Your great-aunt? Not Laura Gavin's boss? Not the great Dame Beatrice?'

'Yes, of course; and, if she can't help us, my Uncle Ferdinand will.'

'Who's he? What could he do?'

'He is Sir Ferdinand Lestrange, Q.C. Appearing for the defence is his main line of country. He loves getting people off, whether they've done it or not.'

'I don't call that ethical.'

'When did ethics have anything to do with the law?'

'Be that as it may, how very well connected you are!'

'We may be glad of it, especially me. I only hope my great-aunt is at home.'

The telephone call was taken by Dame Beatrice herself, for Laura was still in Scotland and not expected back for a day or two. Hermione recognised at once the beautiful voice and said, 'Oh, darling! Thank goodness it's you. Great-aunt, I'm in trouble.'

'What have you done — burnt down the woodland nook of which Laura speaks so highly?'

'Much worse than that. The police think we knocked a girl cyclist down with our car and not only left her dead, but tried to hide the body.'

'Dear me! Is there any substance at all in the story?'

'Of course there isn't. We've never knocked anybody down, let alone killed her. We even went straight to the police and reported finding the body. We should hardly have done that if we were guilty, would we?'

'Conscience doth make cowards of us all.'

'That's what the police think. They think that, after we'd hidden the body, we panicked and went racing off to them to unburden ourselves.'

'Do they suspect simply because you reported the accident?'

'We didn't have any accident. The whole thing was nothing to do with us at all.'

'But the police must have some good reason for suspecting you.'

'That's the worst of it. When I was on my way through the woods to park the car that evening, it skidded and hit a tree.'

'Misfortunes never come singly. You marked the car, I suppose.'

'Yes, not much, but of course it's given the police something to take hold of. Oh, darling, do please come and support us! You couldn't manage to get here by Monday, could you?'

'You may expect me on Sunday afternoon. I shall have George to drive me down. Book two rooms at the hotel nearest to where you are staying and when we meet you must tell me the whole story in detail. Did you yourself see the body?'

'No. The two older ones left Tamsin and me in the car while they went over to look at the bicycle. Then they cast around on the moor in case the girl had wandered off.'

'Why did they think of that?'

'Oh, darling, I don't know. People do wander around when they've had a shock, don't they?'

'People vary in their reactions. However, I suppose your friends' intentions were commendable.'

'She's coming,' said Hermione, emerging from the telephone kiosk and addressing Isobel, who was waiting outside. 'We shall be all right now.'

'Famous last words!' said Isobel. 'Come on and let's see if we can find this tree of yours.'

The Trent's holiday finished on the Saturday, so while Isobel and Hermione were searching for the marked tree, John Trent came to the cabin on a neighbourly visit, probably the last, he explained.

'I hope you've had no more trouble with that lad,' he said.

Oh, no, thanks,' said Erica, who had answered the door.

'Good. One wondered, because one spotted a police car here.'

'Come in and we'll tell you about it.'

'I don't know whether we are at liberty to do that until the police release the story to the press,' said Tamsin.

'Oh, it will come out today. The police haven't told us to keep quiet about it. Besides, that poor girl's friends will be making enquiries by now,' Erica said. 'The fact is we found a girl's body on the moors when we were out yesterday. The police had to be told, so we went to the police station yesterday and they came this morning to ask us a few more questions.'

'Good Lord! The girl was not anybody you knew, I hope.'

'The body? Oh, no. Hermione saw a bicycle through the window of the car and then Isobel and I got out to have a look in case somebody was ill or had had an accident, and a bit further off we found her.'

'How beastly for you!'

'Yes, it was. You see, until the police got this idea that we'd run her down with our car, we thought the escaped convict must have done it, although, if so, it seemed odd that the front wheel of the bike was so badly buckled. Still, he must be desperate for money and food and there was no sign of her handbag or anything else she might have had with her. The police asked whether we had ever seen her before, which I thought was rather a silly question. Tamsin thought she might have come from the Youth Hostel at Long Cove Bay, but it was only a suggestion. Considering that the bike was lying in a slanting position with the buckled front wheel pointing away from our car, either she was cycling on the wrong side of the road or she was going *towards* Long Cove Bay, not away from it.'

'If she'd been hit by a car, the bike could have been knocked clean across the road, I suppose, so you can't prove much by the position of the front wheel.'

'That's true, so it's not much use worrying about the bike. They will have got a doctor to look at the body and if *he* says the girl was knocked down and killed by a car, I expect that's what happened. The trouble is that they think it was *our* car.'

'They surely don't think so just because you reported finding the body?'

'Unfortunately there's more to it than that,' said Tamsin. 'Hermione parked the car after we got back and on the way to the carpark from unloading me here because of my wretched ankle, she had a skid and hit a tree and marked the car. She and my sister are out now, trying to find the tree.'

'Anything I can do to help?'

'I don't think so, thanks,' said Erica. 'Do you mind not mentioning any of this to anybody at present?'

'Trust me.'

'Well, I hope we can,' said Tamsin, when he had gone. 'We don't want the story to be passed round until we know where we stand, do we?'

The other two came back with mixed tidings. The skidmarks were impossible to find because so many cars had used the road to the carpark that any evidence of the kind which Hermione had hoped for was destroyed. Apart from that, she and Isobel had failed to locate a damaged tree.

'I thought I remembered pretty well where I had the skid,' she said, 'but I was only thinking about the bicycle and you two finding the body, so I may be wrong about where the skid took place, and, of course, there are scores of trees.'

'We'll all have another look later on,' said Isobel. 'Anyway, Dame Beatrice Lestrange Bradley is coming on Sunday, so with her at our side the police won't dare to bully us.'

'There's only one trouble about that tree,' said Erica. 'Even if you *do* find it, I can't see how we can prove that it was Hermione's skid that marked it. I don't suppose she's the only driver to have had her wheels slip sideways on wet leaves.'

After this pessimistic observation, lunch was a somewhat silent meal. At one point Tamsin said, 'Are you beginning to wish we had never come to this place?' To this Erica replied with equal pessimism:

'I bet Hermy begins to wish she had never met us.'

'Well,' said the superintendent to Detective-Inspector Ribble, 'the ball is in your court now, Bob. The medical evidence — and Forensic are dead certain to back it up — is that the girl didn't receive fatal injuries by being knocked down by a car. She may have been knocked down, but that she was actually killed by repeated blows on the head is the official verdict. Probably struck from behind with a stone first of all, and then, when she tumbled down, there must have been a frenzied attack on her. Somebody wanted to make quite sure she was dead. We may know more about that when we know who she is. One of those four girls suggested she might have come from the Youth Hostel. Anyhow, the murderer made off with her gear, we think. She must have had at least a handbag, but we searched a wide area and found absolutely nothing, so, up to now, we haven't a clue to her identity.'

'If she was on a solitary holiday and was a Youth Hosteller, sir, she may not be missed for days. Chances are she was a school-teacher, don't you think, sir?'

'Why, Bob?'

'Schools get a week's half-term holiday round about now, sir. I've got three kids, so I know.'

'Oh, yes, of course. Doesn't help us until somebody misses her and comes forward. Even if she taught at a local school there would be nobody there except a caretaker and the chances are that she could have come from absolutely anywhere. We shall put out a description, of course, but I think it's just going to be a question of wait and see. We shall try the Youth Hostel, of course.'

'Even when we know who she is, sir, we shan't be much further forward if this was one of those opportunist, unpremeditated jobs, and that's what it looks like on the face of it, except those sort are usually sex motivated. You seem to have ruled out the chap who absconded a day or two ago. They haven't picked him up yet and he was in for murder, wasn't he?'

'Wife-murder, yes, but he was one of these arsenic operators. This person or these persons who attacked the girl must have gone berserk. It wasn't in keeping with anything that's known about the chap from Hangwood.'

'If a man's desperate enough, sir, you can't guarantee what he'll do.'

'It's the bashing he gave her. That doesn't fit our chap: All he had to do, if it *was* him, was to knock her unconscious and make off with any food or money she was carrying. If she was attacked from behind she wouldn't be able to describe him.'

'Perhaps she put up a fight, sir, and he lost his head.'

'Against that is the theory that if he struck the first blow from behind her, that was the blow which killed her. Even if it didn't, it wouldn't have left her in any condition to put up a fight. I don't think we can query the medical evidence, you know, and that includes one curious little fact.'

'You mean we've got a clue, sir?'

'No such luck, I'm afraid, but it's an odd little circumstance, all the same. The doctors found a mushroom or some kind of toadstool — it hasn't been identified yet — embedded in the head-wound. Wherever that kind grows, it doesn't usually grow on the moors among the heather.'

'Looks as though she was killed in the woods, sir.'

'But who would have taken the body back to the moor to hide it when it would have been much safer and easier to put it in one of the thickets? It looks less and less like our man, to my mind.'

'And those young women, sir?'

'Damned if I know. They do have one of the forest cabins. I think we'll have to keep tabs on them. Even if they are not guilty, they may know something which they haven't told us. There must be *some* explanation of how that fungus came to be embedded in the wound. To go back to our man, though, he may have been fly enough to reason that a buckled bike could have been biffed by a car, and as he can prove he doesn't possess a car . . .'

'That raises a very interesting point, sir. She *could* have been knocked off her bike by a car and so badly hurt that the driver thought he had better put her out of her misery, as though she was a wounded bird. I agree we should not abandon the car aspect, sir. Those four young women might have the humanitarian urge I suggested and also a good big spanner in the boot.'

'Far-fetched, Bob, surely! Young women don't go in for that kind of strong-arm stuff.'

'Women go in for wrestling and soccer and I believe some even play Rugby League football, sir. They do weight-lifting and run the marathon and put the shot. There's only professional boxing and throwing the hammer still closed to them in this country. They drive racing-cars and ride horses on equal terms with men —'

'You sound like a Women's Libber, Bob.'

'Not at all, sir. Just painting the picture, that's all.'

'I can't imagine any of those four young women bludgeoning another young woman to death, not even for the reason you suggested. Besides, not many women could face finishing off a wounded bird.'

'Just as you say, sir. Well, my first job, as I see it, is to do a round of the neighbourhood, including that Youth Hostel just outside Long Cove Bay, to see if anybody knows anything about the dead woman. All the same, sir, I would have thought it more typical of women than of men to have been panicked into trying to hide the body while quite forgetting to hide the bike, and then, in a fresh fit of panic, to rush off to the police and report the death. Don't you think we ought just to keep those possibilities in mind?'

'Keep in mind whatever you like, Bob. I suppose anything is possible. There is just one thing. A chap came in and reported the theft of an anorak and a rucksack from that Youth Hostel. I don't suppose it has any bearing on this case, but it might lead us to this escaper of ours. I would like to clear him out of our way if we can. I don't believe for a moment that he did this job. It's quite untypical of his line of country. He's a poisoner, and a cobbler always sticks to his last.'

'There is that fungus which was pushed into the head-wound,' said Ribble. 'Some toadstools are very poisonous, sir; and he did poison his wife.'

# –6–

# SELF-HEAL

The warden of the Youth Hostel was not pleased at being disturbed before the recognised opening time of five pm, but when she opened her cottage door to Ribble and his detective-sergeant, although she did not recognise them immediately as plain-clothes police officers, she did realise that they were not prospective hostellers calling out of hours.

'Yes?' she said. She had been accompanied to the door by an impressive-looking Alsatian dog which reinforced her single-syllable greeting with one of its own, a short but menacing growl.

Ribble disclosed his official identity and asked for a word. He and his sergeant were invited in, the dog was ordered to retire, and the two men were given seats in what had been the cottage parlour when the building had been the lodge to a private house.

'We are interested in two people who may have stayed at the hostel recently,' said Ribble.

'We get all sorts. What have these two been up to? If it's anything about a missing anorak and a rucksack, I was not told about either. I merely heard the boy saying to his friend that they were gone. Nothing was complained about officially, if you understand me.'

'Did that surprise you?'

'Oh, no, because I knew, and I'm sure *they* knew, who had taken the things. Serve them right, I thought, for having such a friend.'

'They reported the theft at Gledge End headquarters, but that is nothing to do with us, and I don't think those are the two we're making enquiries about. We might possibly be interested in the friend, though. Can you describe him? I suppose you've got his name and address.'

'Oh, yes, we have to keep careful records, of course. Half a minute and I'll get my book. Oh, you want a description. Well, as I said, we get all sorts and so long as they've booked in before-hand by letter and with the fee — we don't accept telephone messages or any *promises* to pay —' she laughed merrily, a very different personality from the stern-looking female accompanied by dog who had answered the door, 'they're in. I don't ever refuse anybody who has kept the rules, especially anybody who looked as if he'd spent the night on the moors in all that rain.'

'Oh, you thought these three had spent the night on the moors, did you?'

'No, only the one you want me to describe.'

'Ah, only the one you think stole the anorak and the rucksack. Now, madam, what did he look like?'

'Nothing on earth, poor man. He was a lot older than the other two. They would have been in their early twenties, I dare say, and quite well-spoken and just the decent, quiet type we like to have. Did *his* share of the chores, too, as well as their own, before they left in the morning.'

'Why was that?'

'Because he must have sneaked out of the hostel before anybody was stirring. By the way, my name is Beck — Mrs — and, as you see, I don't live in the hostel myself. Some wardens do, but they're generally men, I should think. I prefer to keep myself as much out of the way as I can. I think the hostellers prefer it that way and I'm sure I do. I'll tell you another thing: on thinking things over, I don't believe the two younger ones knew this older fellow, else why should he have robbed one of them and then sneaked off like that? Something fishy about him to do a thing like that, wouldn't you say?'

'An older fellow?' said Ribble. 'How much older?'

'Oh, into his fifties I wouldn't wonder, but perhaps looked

older than he really was because of being so wet and tired and dirty, and not being shaved and all that. He would have been a right mean-looking fellow, anyway, and had hardly a word to say for himself.'

'But he was correctly booked in, I think you said.'

'Well, *somebody* was, but I've been wondering whether that somebody was him or somebody else. I'll just fetch the register book. If he was a cuckoo in the nest I can't help it. I can only go by the membership cards they hand in .'

The detective-sergeant politely opened the door for her. They heard her call the dog and then they heard the front door close. Apparently she kept the register over at the hostel itself and not in the cottage.

'Well,' said Ribble, when the sergeant had returned to his seat, 'what do you make of all that?'

'Could be our man, sir.'

'I'll lay a ducat it *is* our man. I'll show her his picture when she gets back. I mean, it all tallies, doesn't it? What with the age, the theft, the mean look, the sleeping rough and getting wet through, it could almost add up, and I'm inclined to bet on it. Well, there's one obvious line of country we can take as soon as we've got the addresses. We can check on all three of these chaps and see what kind of story they have to tell. Before that, though, we'll see whether Mrs Beck can give us any help over this murdered girl. From the fact that she was cycling between this place and Gledge End, I think it's quite possible that she was either coming away or going to the hostel, although, of course, she may have been coming from her own home or been staying at one of the farms.'

'Or in one of the forest cabins, sir, and had been out for a spin on her bike.'

'We can ask, but I doubt whether she was one of the forest lot. She wouldn't have booked one of the cabins all to herself. They are geared to accommodate parties of five or six people with rent appropriate to this number. If she had been a member of such a party, enquiries would have been made about her before now, and we should have found out who she was.'

Upon her return to her cottage Mrs Beck was able to supply

some information. She opened the register, but, before she could say anything, Ribble asked whether either of the younger men had stayed at the hostel on any other occasion.

'No,' she said, 'but I think they had done quite a lot of hostelling. They seemed to the manner born, if you know what I mean. You can always tell the experienced ones. Here we are, look. I didn't have a lot in that night or the night before. Time of year, you know. They mostly come in the summer, not late autumn like this, and in this part of the country.'

'Ah, yes. Now, can you tell me which of the names you have down under this date is that of the older man we require?'

Mrs Beck could help him only a little over this. The bookings had been made and the fees sent by Steve Piggott. The other two were down as Tony Mackie and Bert Leeds, but which was which she had no idea, since Steve had handed in and, at the end of the stay, collected all three membership cards.

'All I know is that Piggott, Mackie and Leeds are the three that came together, as you see by the way I've bracketed them in the book. I know which was Piggott because of the three cards being handled and all the fees paid in by him and him giving his own name to me, but none of them had ever been here before. Piggott wanted to hold some kind of gospel meeting in the common-room, but I said I couldn't permit that, as the common-room was common to all and some members might object. He took it very well. It was a shame he was the one to be robbed, but it's what the innocent must expect, I suppose.'

'There was a photograph on the warning notices we sent out,' said Ribble. 'Couldn't you have compared it with this third man, the scruffy one?'

'Oh, it was very smudgy,' said the warden. 'Besides, he came with the other two, and all three cards handed in together, so I didn't connect anything. Well, you wouldn't, would you? If he'd come alone and without a membership card — but, then, he wouldn't, would he? — I should have suspected something, but with everything seeming to be in order . . .'

Ribble said that he quite understood. He added that it must be very lonely for her in the winter, but it turned out that from the middle of November until the end of February she spent much of her time at her sister's house in Long Cove Bay, returning to open up the hostel only if there happened to be any bookings. These, as she had explained, had to be made in advance, 'I always know where I am, you see,' she said. 'It's all down in writing.'

Ribble said that he was glad to hear it and was relieved that she had the dog. Then he showed her a clear photograph of the convict, but she refused to commit herself.

'Well,' she said, 'if that's all, I generally have a cup of tea about now, before I open up at five for the hostellers. Perhaps you'd join me.'

'Thanks, but there is one other matter, Mrs Beck. I think I mentioned we're interested in two people. One is this escaped convict, the other is a young woman aged somewhere between twenty-five and thirty, of slight build and brown-haired. She was a cyclist and could have been making for this hostel or coming away from it. She was wearing blue jeans, an orange-coloured shirt, a brown pullover, brown shoes and a bright yellow anorak.'

'Oh, dear! You don't mean something's happened to her? Did she have an accident? Is she hurt?'

'Yes, she met with a serious accident. You seem to recognise the description.'

'Oh, good gracious, yes! That's Tyne, Judy Tyne. She was one of the dancers, you know, only she had a tiff with one of the others and took herself off yesterday morning. She's stayed here before. They've all stayed here before. It's half-term holiday for them. Some are teachers and some might be students. They do sword-dances and jigs and sing the old-fashioned country songs. I've sometimes watched them rehearsing. But how bad is Judy? Is she in hospital?'

'No, not in hospital. You say she had a disagreement with one of the others and took herself off?'

'Yes, but I think the rest of them thought she would come back when she'd cooled down. They were booked in for three nights, you see, so she wouldn't have anywhere else to sleep. But what has she got to do with this prisoner you're chasing after?'

'Probably nothing. Now, Mrs Beck, can you tell us something

more about the rest of the party? I shall have to see them all if this girl is the one we think, but it would be useful to know your opinion of them first.'

'Has something happened worse than what you've said?'

'Yes, I'm afraid it has, ma'am. The accident was a fatal one and the evidence suggests that something *more* than what I call an accident may have taken place, so anything you can tell me will be very helpful. Now, ma'am, just give me a line on the other youngsters' He pointed to her entries in her ledger. 'These will be the biggish party that you've also bracketed together, I take it? A very useful procedure on your part, I'm sure. Keeps everything shipshape, eh?'

'That's right. Well, as you can see, there are nine of them. I can't tell you a lot about them. We get all kinds, some rough diamonds, some quite cultured, and them all using the hostel because it's cheap and most of them are young. This lot, the dancers and singers, are the sort that are no trouble at all. I had them last year at this time and I was glad to have them again.'

'You mentioned some kind of disagreement. Did you gather what it was about?'

'No, but I think it was between Judy and another of the girls. *Is* it Judy who is dead? You mean this convict killed her?'

'We don't know. When we get the body identified, I shall be able to tell you more. Don't worry your head at present, ma'am, or begin jumping to conclusions. Just answer the questions, then we shall know where we are. I see that the party booked in on Wednesday.'

'And are allowed three nights, so tonight is their last.'

'Do you know where they are staying after tonight?'

'No, I don't. All I know is that they are giving a concert at Gledge End tomorrow afternoon, but if Judy has left I don't see how they will manage. But this girl you're talking about, oh, it couldn't be Judy! She can't have been murdered, not a respectable girl like her.'

'Well, that's what we're not too sure about,' said Ribble, giving up his comforting tone. 'She seems to have been knocked or dragged off her bicycle, but we can't talk about murder until we know that she wasn't hit by a passing car. On the other hand, her injuries don't really suggest a hit-and-run driver and our knowledge of our bird who is on the run from Hangwood gaol doesn't suggest that he killed the girl who may not be Judy Tyne anyway. He is a convicted murderer, it's true, but he is a poisoner and only of his wife, at that, so —'

'*Only* of his wife? I like that!' exclaimed Mrs Beck, perking up a little. 'Are you married, Inspector?'

'Yes. I didn't mean it quite the way it sounded. I meant that he is most unlikely to murder anybody else, that's all. What I would like you to do is to sum up these dance people for me. You say they have stayed here before and you see so many youngsters that you must be a pretty good judge of them. You mentioned a quarrel, and that, in case of violent death, is something which ought not to be overlooked.'

'I don't want my words to get anybody into trouble.'

'Of course not. Personal opinion is only a very rough guide and can't incriminate anybody. Just fire away. We are very discreet.'

'But the sergeant is going to write down what I say.'

'Nothing but names and addresses. Nothing you tell us can be used in evidence, but it would help me to get a line on these young people. First of all, what about the quarrel which caused Judith Tyne to take herself off? How serious would you say it was?'

'I don't know anything about it, but I think it must have been on account of one of the boys. Giles is the leader, and a very nice boy and I should think very capable. I don't think the quarrel was anything to do with him. Then there is Willie. He is Scottish by birth, tall and dark. He might be the brooding type, but I wouldn't think he bothered much about girls. Probably got a girl of his own back home, anyway. Micky is the youngest and very slight and fair, very like his sister to look at. The others are Ronnie, another nice boy, and then there is Peter. I'm sure Ronnie is much too lazy to bear malice to anybody. I wonder he can even exert himself to dance. He's always saying how tired he is, but he's big and healthy enough. Just bone idle when it comes to pulling his weight, but all the others seem to like him, and I must say I've got a soft spot for him myself.'

'What about Peter?' asked Ribble, checking the names in the book.

'I don't know. He seems very quiet and sort of nondescript, if you know what I mean. Keeps himself to himself. He's the artistic one and very clever at making things.'

'Could he be a dark horse, do you think?'

'I really couldn't say. I shouldn't think he has enough character to be anything very much, but you never know, do you? Look at Doctor Crippen.'

'Ah,' said Ribble, looking alert. 'You connect Peter with Doctor Crippen, do you?'

'Good gracious, no! Who ever heard of such a thing? Don't you put words into my mouth that I never intended!'

'I'm sorry, ma'am. Well, what about the last of the boys?'

'They call him Plum. He's big-made and very much a man. He could be the oldest of them, as a matter of fact. I've nothing to tell you about him except my dog doesn't like him.' Upon this, the warden burst into tears. 'Oh, dear! Oh, dear!' she sobbed. 'I knew no good would come of all that fussing over Mick.'

Ribble waited and then, as she calmed herself, he repeated what she had said, but put it in the form of a question.

'No good would come of all this fussing over Mick?' he said.

'Yes. There were the three of them, you see. Well, Willie is a boy, so he hardly counted, if you know what I mean, but the other two, Judy and Peggy, they were always going out of their way to treat him as if he was like a delicate piece of china and might get broken if they weren't extra careful. Not that there was anything I would have called delicate about him. So far as I could see, he may have looked slim and pretty — more like a girl in some ways — but he could dance the legs off the rest of them, I reckon, and from the extras he bought at the hostel shop I don't think there was anything wrong with his appetite.'

'But the two girls thought him fragile? What about the boys?' You mentioned Willie. What about the others?'

'Treated him just like one of themselves and used to joke with him about Judy and Peggy. If you ask me, he liked the fuss the girls made of him. Boys do like having a fuss made of them, don't they? I suppose it starts with their mothers.'

'To put it clearly, ma'am,' said Sergeant Nene, 'were both the girls in love with him?'

'Oh, no,' she replied without hesitation. 'It was nothing like that. He was so young, you see, compared to the other boys. He was younger than his sister, but so very much like her to look at that you'd think she would get the same treatment, but nobody ever spoilt Pippa. She seemed always a bit apart from the others, I always thought, and wasn't really very interested in the dancing, but only in the music.'

'Well, thank you for your help, ma'am. There is one more thing you can do for us if you will. It will take us a little time to establish the identity of this dead girl unless you will help us. If she *isn't* Judy Tyne I shall be glad; if she *is*, well, we shall have saved a lot of time.'

'She's Judy. I know it in my bones,' said the warden, this time looking grim instead of becoming tearful, 'and if there is anything I can do to help catch whoever killed her I shall do it. It means the mortuary, I suppose. If it *is* Judy I must tell the others. It would come better than from a stranger.'

'Would you be prepared to make the identification now, Mrs Beck?' asked Ribble.

'I should have to get back in time to open up.'

'Nothing easier, if we go at once.'

'Does it mean I'll have to speak at the inquest?'

'Not if it's the girl we think. We'll get a more formal identification from her relatives, if she's got any. Not to worry about the inquest. Shall we go?'

Mrs Beck nerved herself for the ordeal, but it was over in a matter of seconds. She had no doubt about identifying the dead girl as Judy Tyne.

'Oh, well, she'll have no more troubles, poor girl,' she said, 'but get that villain you must, and then I'll sleep at night.'

# −7−

# WILD THYME (1)

The little band of musicians and dancers who billed themselves under the name of Wild Thyme had been nine in number (as the warden had stated) before the death of the companion who was known to them as Judy. There were the fair-haired Giles, the dark Scot Willie, brawny Plum, the slim, girlish-looking, agile Mick, the artist Peter and the good-natured, easy-going, rather lazy Ronnie. These were the morris dancers. The three girls provided most of the music, but Judy and Peggy teamed up with Giles, Ronnie and Plum for such folk-dances as called for a team of three men and three women, the third girl being impersonated by Mick in print frock and fichu, while Peter took over the violin-playing from Peggy and, if there was a piano available (as more often than not there was) Willie played the accompaniment to Pippa's flute.

Judy, the dead girl, had played a small concertina, and in addition to playing the flute and the violin, both Pippa and Peggy could act as accompanists on the piano if they were called upon to do so, and so could others.

Peter's artistic talents were of considerable value to the company. He was the male equivalent of wardrobe mistress and in addition to having an eye for colour and the general effect of the costumes, he was particularly successful at designing any 'props' which might be needed for the dances and folk-songs which were the main items in the company's repertoire. Thus, for the final dance, he had made a terrifying outfit for the hobby-horse based on the wicker-work processional figure called Snap the Dragon, which he had seen in a Norwich museum and adapted to a ferocious-looking design of his own. In addition, and for the end of the dance, which terminated in ritual slaughter, he had made a horrifying bloody head which was triumphantly displayed by the leader as the company performed the last figure of the dance.

At just after five o'clock on the Friday afternoon of Ribble's visit to the Youth Hostel, the company, who had been rehearsing in the church hall over at Gledge End for the following day's performance, came back and were met by Mrs Beck, who, having been returned by Ribble from the mortuary, took Giles, the leader, over to her cottage to break to him the news of Judy's death.

'And the police will be here again,' she said, 'so you had better warn the others. The inspector seems a nice man, but you never know with the police.'

Giles' reactions to the news were two-fold. He felt and expressed shock and grief, but on the way back from the cottage to the hostel his mind was already busy with his own concerns. To himself he said, 'Well, thank goodness it isn't one of the morris men! We can manage the music, but Mick will have to stand in for Judy and the folk dances will have to be done by us men, unless we leave them out altogether, but, if we do, it's going to make a big hole in the programme. Perhaps we ought to cancel tomorrow's show. No, too late for that. We shall have to go through with it somehow.'

'Why did she want you?' asked Plum, when the company had settled to their meal of baked beans and pork sausages.

'Tell you later,' said Giles, who found that shock and grief, contrary to popular belief, can put a keen edge on the appetite. 'We'll take an hour's rest after this, just to settle our stomachs, and then we've got to go over what we rehearsed this afternoon.'

'Judy really has walked out on us, then?'

'She won't be coming back, that's for sure.' When they had spent the hour lying on their bunks, he called them into the common-room. 'We have to carry on with tomorrow's show,' he said. 'We've sold the tickets and the money has been promised to the Spastics Society. We can't back out now.'

'Judy said she would rather die than stay with us,' observed Pippa. 'It makes you think a bit, doesn't it? Tempting providence, I mean, and all that.'

'Oh, shut up!' said Peggy, knowing that it was the quarrel with her which had precipitated Judy's departure.

'What we've got to think about is that ending to Kirkby Moorside,' said Plum. 'That sword dance is one of our high spots and it loses a lot if there's no victim.'

'Oh, Peggy can do that,' said Peter. 'We didn't rehearse it this afternoon, but she's only got to run into the circle after we've made the knot and then fall down dead when we draw the swords out.'

'I couldn't get into the costume,' protested Peggy. 'I'm taller and bigger than Judy.'

'Then Mickie will have to do it,' said Plum. 'He looks lovely in drag and he can do a beautiful death-fall, can't you, Mick?'

' "Nay, faith, let me not play a woman; I have a beard coming",' said the graceful juvenile.

'You were marvellous in the folk dances this afternoon, when there were only the five of us. Never made any muddles,' said Plum, 'but then there's the Irish jig. I must have a partner for that and Mickie can't do everything.'

'Well, can't Peggy let the Irish costume out?' said Ronnie. 'It doesn't matter whether the victim in the sword dance is a man or a woman, but the Irish jig needs a man and a girl, doesn't it?'

'Even if Peggy could adapt the costume, she can't do the jig,' said Giles.

'Why not? She knows the steps. We all do.'

'The Irish jig needs a fiddler and she is the only one we've got.'

'What's the matter with the piano in the church hall? It's in tune.'

'You can't have a piano accompaniment for the Irish jig,' said

Peggy. 'It would be most inartistic. Besides, that costume is down to raw edges already. You can't possibly let it out enough to fit me.'

'So that's settled,' said Giles, 'and good old Mickie will have to save the show. Good on yer, Mick, me old cobber!' He patted him encouragingly on the back.

'Well,' said Mick dubiously, 'I'll do what I can if the Kirkby Moorside dress and the Irish jig costume fit me, but . . .'

'We'll see they do,' Peter promised him. 'They'll be a tiny bit short on you, but you've got lovely legs.'

'Will you fit me up with whatever I wear underneath them, Pippa?'

'You shall have my personal slip, pants and built-up bra,' said Pippa. Nobody had suggested that she should stand in for Judy. 'She's a good tootler on the flute,' as one of the men put it, 'but, when it comes to the light fantastic, she has two left feet and trips over both of them.'

'Are you certain Judy won't come back?' asked Mick. 'Did she take her hostel membership card back from Ma Beck when she lit out for the wide open spaces?'

'I didn't think to ask, but it doesn't matter now.'

'But if she did take back her card she'll have nowhere to sleep. We're not booked in at the other hostel until tomorrow night,' said Pippa.

'It doesn't matter,' said Giles again. The others looked at him.

'Well, spill it,' said Plum. 'She isn't coming back. That's clear. Why isn't she?'

'Something's happened to her.' said Peggy, somewhat hysterically, 'and it's my fault! It's all my fault! She's met with an accident! She's in hospital She's had an accident and fallen off her bike. She went belting off at such a rate that anything could have happened to her.'

'Yes, it's happened to her,' said Giles. 'She won't be coming back because she's dead.'

Ribble showed up at Mrs Beck's cottage again at half-past six and asked whether the troupe had been given the news of Judy's death.

'I told the leader,' she replied,' and he will have told the others by now.' She took the inspector over to the hostel just as the shocked company was about to begin the rehearsal upon which Giles insisted. Ribble summed them up and made his own announcement. It was received in mixed fashion. Pippa, who had been crying, burst into tears again. Her girlish-looking brother put his arm round her and said nothing. Giles said, 'O Lord! The police!' Plum said, 'If only she'd stayed with us!' Ronnie found Peter's hand and squeezed it so hard in his emotion that Peter, with an oath indicative of pain, wrenched the crushed fingers from his neighbour's grasp and massaged them. He said, 'She knew about the convict on the moor. There was a notice up.' Willie agreed, but added, 'It was a car. Must have been.' Peggy said, 'I never meant to quarrel with her,' and joined in with Pippa's tears.

Judging, from these reactions, that Plum and Giles were the least emotionally affected, Ribble decided to interview them first.

'Perhaps, sir,' he said to Giles, 'you would accompany me to Mrs Beck's cottage, where she has placed her sitting-room at my disposal. She will remain with the rest of the party over here. You, sir,' he addressed Plum, 'will come across when this gentleman returns. As the matter may turn out to be more serious than a road accident, I shall be obliged if, on your return from the cottage, neither of you discusses what has been said there until I have spoken with every one of your party.'

'Is that the reason for bringing Mrs Beck over?' asked Giles. 'To make sure they keep their mouths shut, I mean.'

'Yes, sir. At any rate, it is one reason,' Ribble replied, 'and the same applies to the rest of you.'

'I say!' said Peter. 'I don't like this! Shouldn't we have a lawyer present or something?'

'As you wish, sir, but you will appreciate that if this death was not caused by a hit-and-run driver — and I have reasons for keeping an open mind about that — to insist upon having your lawyer present would hamper my enquiries because, by the time you had got in touch with him, a good deal of police time would have been lost and possible clues might have been destroyed.'

'Oh, don't be an ass, Peter,' said Giles. 'Do you want the inspector to think *you* did it? Lawyers indeed!'

'Now, sir,' said Ribble, when he had taken him across to Mrs Beck's cottage and the warden had remained in the hostel commonroom, 'perhaps you would give me an account of the circumstances which led to the young lady going off alone on her bicycle yesterday.'

'I don't want to say anything against her now she's dead.'

'Anything you *say* against her will hardly be as shocking as what somebody has *done* against her, sir, and may help me to apprehend this party of the second part. Either he is a cowardly and utterly callous motorist, or else, as we are inclined to suspect, we have to look for a deliberate murderer. I shall be grateful for anything you can tell me. The circumstances of this girl's death must be cleared up, so — the whole truth, if you please, sir.'

'Yes, all right, then. Well, I ought to explain that Judy was almost a newcomer to the gang. She was a replacement, in fact, for Cynthia.' Abandoning his first attitude, Giles went into detailed explanations. There had to be nine people in the troupe. Nine was a magic and mystical number in folklore. There were the Nine Muses, the Nine Men's Morris, the Nine Stones of Winterborne Abbas, ninepins, the nine gods of the Etruscans, the nine Worthies, the nine points of the law, Milton's nine enfolded spheres, the nine days of Deucalion's ark before it was stranded on Mount Parnassus.

Ribble let him go on, realising that the young man was under more strain than he had thought. Giles continued his recitation.

'Then there are "dressed up to the nines",' he said, 'and the nine earths with Hela the Norse goddess of the ninth one, and there are nine Orders of angels, not to mention the nine virgin goddesses of the ancient Gallic religion, the nine days it took the rebellious angels to fall from heaven, the nine fairies of the Armorica, the nine serpents worshipped in Southern India, the nine-headed Hydra, the nine lives of a cat and the cat o'nine tails — tell me,' he interrupted himself, 'is one of us suspected?'

'Suspected, sir?'

'Oh, come now, Inspector! You wouldn't be wasting your time

with us if you even suspected that Judy was killed by a hit-and-run car. You said as much. Do you think one of us is a murderer?'

'All I need to find out at present, sir, is how the deceased came to be cycling alone when she was a member of your company. According to Mrs Beck there had been some cause for disagreement between two of the young ladies.'

'Good Lord! It wasn't serious enough for Peggy to have done Judy any harm.'

'Probably not, sir, but I should like to hear about it. When did the disagreement take place?'

'Last Wednesday; two days ago. It wasn't about anything much, but you know what girls are. They fly off the handle for anything or nothing. This was all about the hornpipe.'

'The hornpipe, sir?'

'Yes. You see we are always trying to put new things into our show, so Peter suggested this sailors' hornpipe, and everybody thought it a good idea, catchy and sort of patriotic, if you know what I mean. I mean jolly Jack tars and all that. It was to follow a couple of sea shanties we were all going to sing. I think the real trouble was that Peggy was to play the fiddle for the hornpipe, whereas Judy thought her concertina would be better.'

'Are you telling me that this was the first time the two young ladies had fallen out, sir?'

'Well, they never did get along very well together. This was only one of a number of skirmishes. There was really nothing in it at all, but Judy decided to make an issue of it and took herself off on Thursday morning.'

'So the quarrel was on Wednesday. How did you yourself spend Thursday?'

'Plum and I went on our bikes to Gledge End to confirm the arrangements for tomorrow's show.'

'Did you catch up with or pass Judy?'

'No, but I expect we were on a different road. A number of roads from here lead across the moors.'

'Only one, sir, from near the hostel.'

'Oh, you mean the turning as you go towards Long Cove Bay. We went right into the town and took the main Gledge End road from there. It's a better surface and more direct. Where was Judy when — when it happened?'

'Near a turning to the village of Wayland, which is on the border of the Forestry Commission's property. At what time did you get to Gledge End, sir?'

'I don't know exactly. We didn't rush things. When we got to the town we had a bite to eat and then we went to the church hall and arranged the chairs ready for our show. We don't use a stage, you see. We make a hollow rectangle to dance in and put three rows of chairs round to enclose it, so there was a quite a bit of work for us to do and we were at it until about three o'clock. Then we cycled back along the road by which we had come and got in just before the others turned up.'

'Did you expect that Judy would think better of her departure and turn up again that evening?'

'We thought she might have done, because otherwise we couldn't see where she was going to sleep. We're not booked in anywhere else until tomorrow night, but of course we didn't know that it was impossible for her to come back.'

'Well, that's all for the present. Will you send me the gentleman who went with you to Gledge End?'

'I say, are you going to question us one by one?'

'Such is my intention, sir. Why?'

'Well, you see, we simply *must* have a rehearsal tonight to make sure people can fill in for Judy. You know the saying, *the show must go on*. We've sold the tickets, you see, and it's far too late to call the thing off.'

'I shall be as expeditious as I can, sir, but surely you rehearsed earlier today at Gledge End?'

Giles's return to the hostel was greeted with a barrage of questions.

'Did he grill you?'

'Is it third-degree stuff?'

'What sort of things does he ask?'

'He wants to see Plum next,' shouted Giles above the other voices. 'And for goodness' sake,' he added, 'don't spin out the interviews, or we shall never get our rehearsal. He wants to see all of us in turn. It will take all night if you argue, so tell him what he wants to know and don't embroider it.'

All that Ribble wanted from Plum was confirmation of what Giles had told him. He was careful to ask no leading questions, but Plum's answers were all in agreement with the approximate times which Giles had given him, the route the two of them had taken to get to Gledge End and the way they had occupied themselves when they had arrived there. Ribble soon dismissed him and asked him to send over the girl who had quarrelled with Judy.

Peggy was very much on the defensive and began by blurting out the bald question: 'You think somebody murdered Judy, don't you?'

'We have to keep all possibilities in mind, miss.'

'Well, it certainly wasn't one of us.'

'If you would just answer one or two questions, miss, bearing in mind that nobody has been accused of murder or anything of the kind. My object is to eliminate, not to accuse. Now I would like to know exactly how you spent Thursday.'

'I went to the hairdresser's in Broadsands.'

'You were hardly there all day, miss.'

'It took me an hour and a half to cycle there and an hour and a half to cycle back, half an hour for a café lunch and an hour in the hairdresser's.'

'Can you give me the name of the hairdresser, miss?'

'Yes. It is Antoine's in Duke Street. I always go there. The assistant I always have is called Marcelle. Does that satisfy you?'

'Thank you, miss.'

'I suppose you've heard that I had a row with Judy on Wednesday. Well, we did have a few words and she took offence and went off in a temper on Thursday, but we all thought she would come back, although Giles put in a rehearsal on Thursday evening just in case.'

'So you went nowhere near Gledge End on Thursday, miss?'

'Of course not. I cycled into Long Cove Bay and then turned north for Broadsands. I didn't go anywhere near Gledge End.'

'May I ask why you quarrelled with Judy?'

'It wasn't so much a quarrel; just an argument. One thing led to another. It always does. It was about the music for the horn-pipe at first and then it sort of hotted up and Mick got involved.'

'You mean he joined in the argument?'

'No. Judy and I both had a mother-complex about him. He's only nineteen and really more like a girl than a boy. You feel protective towards him. We both did, but it didn't bring us together. Quite the reverse, in fact.'

'May I put a question which is not directly concerned with the matter at issue, miss? Do you and the rest depend upon your performances for earning a living?'

'Good gracious, no! Some of us are teachers on half-term holiday, Mick is on strike from a factory office, and Judy was married and ran a play-school. Any money we make goes mostly in expenses and anything over goes to charity. Mostly we only put on a Saturday show, and that's what we're going to do in Gledge End. We're really simply on holiday, cycling and walking and staying at the hostels.'

'Would you know Judy's home address? She was not wearing a wedding-ring when we found her. What was her married surname?'

'She was Mrs Tyne, But I don't know the address. I expect Giles does. He's secretary as well as leader, so she was sure to be in his book. Running a play-school she would have to be on the telephone, too. He probably knows the number.'

'Thank you for your help, miss. Would you kindly ask the youngest gentleman to come over here?'

Mick was nervous. Ribble tried to put him at ease.

'Just a few questions, sir,' he said. 'Perhaps only one , in fact, will be necessary. Will you tell me exactly how you spent Thursday?'

'Thursday? That's the day it happened.'

'The death? Yes, that's right, sir.'

'I feel responsible, you know.'

'Why is that, sir?'

'The row, the disagreement, you know.'

'I wouldn't worry about that, sir. Just tell me where you went and what you did on that day.'

'Willie and I have a tandem.' (Ribble had seen one among the bicycles in the shed.) 'We went to Crosswell on it.'

'Was it customary for your party to break up in that way, sir?'

'How do you mean?'

'It was not your custom to remain together on the days when you were not performing?'

'Quite often we did stick together, but there was this row between the two girls, you see, and anyway Plum and Giles thought they ought to go over to Gledge End to make sure everything was all right for Saturday.'

'But the rest of you saw no reason why you should go with them?'

'They said they didn't need any help. Of course, they hadn't thought about having to rearrange all the seating. We usually perform on Saturday mornings in school halls, you see, and the school arranges the chairs the way we want them before the kids go home on Friday.'

'So you and Willie cycled to Crosswell on your tandem. A good long stretch, wasn't it?'

'Not on a tandem. We left at soon after nine and got back at six or thereabouts, and, of course, we didn't hitch on the trailer which carries the dance things.'

'Did you know before you started that Mrs Judy Tyne had decided to leave the party?'

'We knew she had threatened it, yes. She said so the night before while the row was on. It was the night we got here. We're only allowed three nights at the same hostel, so it was to be Wednesday, Thursday and tonight here, then the afternoon show tomorrow at Gledge End and then the night at the next Youth Hostel and back to our own homes on Sunday.'

'So what did you and Willie do in Crosswell?'

'We had a rather slap-up meal to which Willie treated me, and then I'm afraid all we did was to go to the cinema. Willie said we needed a rest before we did the ride back.'

'Now let me get this straight, sir. You left the hostel at soon after nine, cycled thirty miles to Crosswell, had a meal — how long did the lunch take?'

'About an hour, I suppose. We got to the cinema just before it opened at two o'clock.'

'And left at what time?'

'I don't know.'

'Did you sit through the whole programme?'

'I don't know. I always go to sleep at the pictures, and the same when I'm watching television. All I know is that Willie woke me when the lights went up and said we had better be moving.'

'You must have *some* idea of what time it was when you left the cinema.'

'Afraid not, no. It was still quite light, if that's any help.'

'To get to Crosswell you would need to go by way of Gledge End, wouldn't you?'

'Not really. We took the narrow road this side of Long Cove Bay, so we by-passed the town.'

'In that case you would have passed the spot where Mrs Tyne was killed. I may as well tell you that, sir.'

'But we would have been *miles* ahead of her, Inspector. We can kick hell out of our tandem and anyway we left the hostel before she did and did not stop anywhere until we got to Cross well.'

'Quite so, sir, I would like you to stay here while I go over to the hostel.'

'Willie will confirm my story, you know.'

'No doubt he will, sir. By the way, Mrs Tyne was quite a gener- ously built lady, was she not?'

'Generously built? You must be joking, Inspector. She was as thin as I am, but not quite so tall. One of our problems is that Peggy can't get into Judy's dance costumes and Pippa can't dance. Are you trying to trick me? You've seen her body, haven't you?'

Ribble was not gone long. Willie confirmed Mick's story in every particular, so the inspector took Peter and Ronnie back with him to the cottage and put one more question to Mick before he released him.

'Which restaurant did you and Willie patronise in Grosswell, sir?'

'Oh, we went to the *Anchor* and sat at the table in the far window on the left as you go in. I'm sure they'll remember us — Willie sent back the soup because it wasn't hot enough.'

'Quite a useful alibi if one is needed,' thought Ribble. Peter and Ronnie could offer no more help than the others had been able to give. They had left the hostel a little later than anybody else, and had cycled north-east to a holiday resort called Stoneship where there was an indoor heated swimming pool with its own restaurant and a hall for table-tennis. There they claimed to have spent the entire day.

All the stories would need to be confirmed by independent witnesses, Ribble decided. He dismissed the young men and asked them to send Pippa to him.

# −8−

# MAIDEN PINK

'There's a lot I've got to tell you,' said Pippa.

'Yes, miss?'

'You don't really think one of us killed Judy, do you?'

'I have to look at all the possibilities, miss.'

'But what about that convict who escaped?'

'It wasn't his kind of murder. He poisoned his wife. He isn't the violent type. We warned people that he was on the loose, but that was so that we could get information which would lead to us being able to catch him. It wasn't because we thought he would attack anybody.'

'Not if he wanted money or food?'

'Ah, that might be another matter. Now, miss, what did you want to tell me?'

'Oh, aren't you going to grill me?'

'I should soon be in serious trouble if I did that, miss. There is just one question. Will you tell me exactly how you spent Thursday?'

'Oh, yes, of course.' Pippa searched his good-tempered, pleasant face, turning large, serious, dark eyes on him. She was very much like Mick, he thought, without being in the least degree pretty. He put her down as being about twenty years old, but in fact she was twenty-six. 'I left the hostel on foot at just before ten,' she said, 'and spent the day with my friends.'

'Where was this, miss?'

'At the nearest farm. It belongs to some people called Ramsgill. It's only about a mile and a half from here, so I didn't take my bicycle. I thought the walk would do me good.'

'So you got to the farm before eleven, miss.'

'Oh, yes. I suppose I was there quite by half-past ten.'

'Were they expecting you?'

'Not exactly, but — well, no, they were not expecting me. I got to know them earlier on in the year when I was researching folk music. Mr Ramsgill's father was living with them and I had heard on the grapevine that he knew a local version of *Heather on the Moor*, so I went long to ask him to sing it to me, which he did. They told me to drop in whenever I was in the neighbourhood, so when the others all had plans for the day and Judy went off in a temper after her row with Peggy, I thought of the farm and walked over there. Of course there were two things I didn't know, but even if I *had* known I think I would still have gone.'

'I can guess one of them, but not the other, and I don't suppose either of them would have anything to do with my enquiry, would it, miss?'

'No, of course not, but, for what they are worth, I didn't know old Mr Ramsgill had died only the month before, and I didn't know that a lodger had taken his place in the spare bedroom.'

'Did you meet this lodger, miss?'

'Oh, yes. He wanted to take me out on the back of his motorcycle, but I explained that it was Mrs Ramsgill I had come to see. When she went out of the room to see about lunch he offered to show me his room, but of course I didn't let him. I think he thought I was younger and greener than I am. I didn't take to him much. I sold him a ticket for our show, though. That was before he asked me to go upstairs with him. We just sat and talked until Mrs Ramsgill came back and then he told her he would get his lunch in Long Cove Bay, so she and I had lunch when Mr Ramsgill came in, and I stayed to tea and walked back to the hostel.'

'So you spent several hours at the farm?'

'Yes. I didn't leave until nearly half-past five.'

'And you did not go out from the farmhouse until you walked back to the hostel?'

'That's right. Mrs Ramsgill and I had a good long gossip. I asked her how she came to have a lodger and she said it was only a temporary thing. He had come last Tuesday afternoon and asked to stay for the rest of the week. He said he was on holiday and had put in a night at the hostel. He didn't like it much and didn't want to stay any longer, but he wanted to remain in the neighbourhood. Well, she had the spare room and he seemed quiet and was well-spoken, so she took him. She said she missed having somebody else in the house after her father-in-law died, and thought this boy would be company for her, but on Tuesday he hired this motorbike and she saw very little of him. He used to take sandwiches or something else to eat and stayed out all day. On Wednesday night he didn't come back at all. He told her next day that the motorcycle had broken down and left him stranded in Wayland Forest, where one of the cabin holiday-makers had given him a bed and dried his clothes for him.'

'And you met him the next day, miss, on Thursday?'

'Yes.'

'I shall have to look him up. If he was out on the moor on Thursday he may have seen something of Mrs Tyne. You wouldn't know how he got his motorbike repaired so quickly, I suppose?'

'No. Mrs Ramsgill told me about the way he stayed out all night because it had broken down, but he certainly had it when I visited the farm on Thursday. I saw it there before he rode off on it. He was very hurt when I wouldn't go with him.'

'It's a point of no importance unless he spotted Mrs Tyne, but at what time did he leave the farm on Thursday? You said he did not have the midday meal there.'

'I should think he went off at about twelve.'

'He will still be at the farm, then, if he was staying a week. Now, miss, what can you tell me about the quarrel between the two ladies?'

'Oh, dear! It doesn't seem very nice to talk about Judy's quarrels now that she's dead, does it?'

'If you could consult her, miss, she might like it to be known who killed her and whether it was by accident or design.'

'Oh, I hadn't thought of it like that. Oh, well, I'll tell you what I can, then. They never did get on, Judy and Peggy. They got across one another almost as soon as Judy joined us. I suppose, being married and running the play-school and all that, she thought herself superior to Peggy, who wasn't married and taught in a rather tatty little school where she thought her talents were wasted. I asked her once why she didn't apply for a better job. She said she had an invalid mother who owned the house they lived in and refused to move. She said her brother and his wife had the old lady for a fortnight in the summer and the October half-term week, but wouldn't take on more than that because she was so cantankerous and upset the children, so Peggy had to cope. It didn't make her very easy to get on with and she and Judy were always at loggerheads, especially over Mickie. They both wanted to mother him, goodness knows why. He's my brother, but I got sick of minding him when he was little.'

'Sisters have a hard time, miss. What was the cause of this last quarrel between the two ladies? The same thing?'

'I don't know. Something must have been said and they simply flew at one another — not physically, of course. I believe Peggy made a remark about Judy's husband and Judy took exception. I don't think they live together. Judy didn't talk about him. Once she told me that she ran the play-school because she had no children of her own, but I didn't like to ask any questions. You don't, do you? — but perhaps it accounted for her feelings about Mick. She almost tried to adopt him, you know.'

'Apart from her relationship with Miss Peggy, would you have called her a happy girl?'

'Well, she wasn't so much of a girl, you know. She was really very mature and I'm bound to say that she was very bossy. I didn't much mind, but, of course, Peggy did. I expect her mother bossed her and she resented it and wasn't going to put up with it from anybody else.'

'How did the men get on with her?'

'With Peggy?'

'No, with Mrs Tyne.'

'Oh, all right, I think. Except for Mickie, who rather disliked being ordered about and having her take a motherly interest in him — he isn't interested in women, only in Willie, whom he absolutely adores — Judy wasn't bossy with the others, and she was very useful as a member of the team. She was awfully good on the concertina and she was a good folk-dancer. Her speciality was Three Meet which she used to do with Giles and Ronnie and she and Peggy used to do a very nice Parsons Farewell with Peter and Plum. Oh, yes, we shall miss her. That's why we need the rest of this evening to do some more rehearsing. Could you let me go back to the hostel now?'

'Certainly, miss, if you will just check one or two points with me. You said you went on foot to the farm. I should have thought that, for a distance of a mile and a half each way, it would have been worth using your bike.'

'I preferred to walk.'

'I wonder if you see, miss, what my check-up means? Everybody except you seems to have cycled to their distinations yesterday, including Mrs Tyne, although she, poor young lady, never got to wherever she was heading for. Well, now, she may have been struck by a passing car. The chances are that that is what happened; on the other hand, when I get the pathologist's report, another theory may emerge. Meanwhile I can't waste time. I must take all possibilities into account and one possibility is that Mrs Tyne was deliberately murdered.'

'Yes, I realise that. I mean I realise that the police have to go into that sort of thing. I can see what you're getting at, too. Anybody on a bicycle might have caught up with Judy and killed her. If I didn't use my machine, the chances are that I couldn't have caught up with her. But I would never dream of killing anybody, Inspector, really I wouldn't.'

'Of course not, miss, but my argument stands as you have stated it. If I find somebody who will swear that your bicycle remained in the hostel shed all day yesterday, then I can wipe you off my slate and very glad I shall be to do so, as much for my own sake as for yours. Did you know that Miss Peggy went to the hair-dresser's?'

'Yesterday? But she couldn't have done.'

'Oh? Why not, miss?'

'Because she had her hair done on Wednesday, before we biked from the other hostel to this one.'

'Perhaps she wasn't satisfied with the result, miss.'

'Why did you ask me about the hairdresser?'

'Because Miss Peggy made what I thought was a rather strange statement, but I am not prepared to disclose what it was, just at present. Well, I think that's all for now. When you go over to the hostel, would you kindly let Mrs Beck know that I have concluded my interviews and that her cottage is at her disposal again?'

He was not quite ready, however, to vacate the cottage. When Mrs Beck came over, he asked whether she could remember the order in which her guests had left and returned to the hostel on the previous day. It was a throwaway question, for he attached no particular importance to her answer. He had asked merely to disguise the real importance of his next query.

She replied that she had no idea of the order in which the party had left and returned. When she went over at ten in the morning to lock up, everybody had gone out, and when she unlocked the hostel door at five in the afternoon, nobody had returned, but must have come in later.

'The accommodation for the three nights had all been paid for, that being the rule,' she said, 'and I held the membership cards until people checked out, which, with this lot, is to be before ten tomorrow morning. There was no reason for me to go over there until the regulation times.'

'Do you happen to know whether they all went off on their bicycles yesterday?'

'All but one. When I had locked up the hostel in the morning I also locked the bicycle shed and there was one bike left in it. The open shed is there for anybody to sit in who comes early before I've opened up at five and I don't mind if sheep stray in there, because it can always be one of the departure chores to clean it out if necessary. The hostellers have to do all the chores, as you probably know. I have to leave that shed open because it's only three-sided. The bicycle shed is a different matter entirely. Bicycles can be a temptation, so if one is in there I lock the door.'

'Yes. Did you happen to notice whether it was a gentleman's or a lady's model which was left behind?'

'No, I didn't notice. Oh, yes, I did, though. It must have belonged to one of the girls because it had a rather fancy shopping-basket on the handlebars.'

'And nobody could have got at it until you unlocked the shed?'

'Nobody. If they get back before five they just prop up their cycles against the side of the shed — I've got the only key — and then sit in the open shed until I unlock the hostel door.'

Ribble's day was not yet over. Mildly pleased to think that he could cross the soulful-eyed Pippa off his list, he decided, all the same, to check her story with Mrs Ramsgill at the farm, although he had no doubt that the two accounts would tally. There was also the chance that at that time in the evening the lodger Pippa had mentioned would be in and available for questioning.

There seemed no doubt about Pippa's innocence. She had come to the farm and departed from it at approximately the times she had stated and within those times she had been in company with the farmer's wife. Unless she had found some means of transport and unless the farmer's wife was lying (which, in the circumstances, seemed most unlikely) there was no way in which she could have got to the spot where the body was found and back again to the hostel at a reasonable time. The lodger, Adam Penshaw, could testify to the time of her arrival but not of her departure, so at the hostel he saw Giles again.

'At what time yesterday did the girl you call Pippa get in?'

Giles looked surprised.

'Pippa?' he said. 'Yesterday? I'm afraid I can't tell you. That's to say, I don't remember.'

'Well, was she in when you yourself got back from Gledge End, sir?'

'I believe not, but she couldn't have been much after Plum and me. She was at supper all right. I remember she asked whether we ought to save anything for Judy, in case Judy got over the row she'd had with Peggy and came back. Oh, and she was babbling about some chap she'd met at the farm. I think she spent the day there. We got to know them last year when we were here. Eggs and things, you know.'

'I suppose she stayed at the farm all the time?'

'How do you mean?'

'She mentioned a young chap who was staying there who had a motorbike. Would that be the chap you referred to?'

'Oh, yes,that's right. I gather he made a bit of a pass at her and then wanted to take her out riding pillion, but she didn't fancy him.'

'So he gave up the idea, did he?'

'He went off on it, she said, and she saw no more of him.'

'Do you know anything about Mrs Tyne's husband, sir?'

Again Giles looked surprised.

'Only that he died two years ago. I went with Judy to the funeral. They hadn't lived together for months, but she thought she ought to go.'

Pleased to get rid of one suspect, Ribble went back to the farm.

'Adam?' said Mrs Ramsgill. 'Yes, he's in. He's in the parlour. The motorbike? Oh, it kept going wrong, so he took it back to where he hired it and turned it in.'

In the parlour Ribble came to the point without beating about the bush.

'This motorbike you hired, sir.'

'What about it?'

'Where did you go when you went out on it yesterday?'

'Why do you want to know? If there's been any trouble about a motorbike, it certainly wasn't mine.'

'I would like to know where you went, that's all, sir.'

'Oh, I just followed my nose as usual.'

'Please be more specific, sir.'

'I did a sort of round trip over the moors.'

'Yes, sir?'

'Well, that's all I can tell you. I went into Long Cove Bay and ate my sandwiches outside the Bull there, went inside for a beer and then I took the main road towards Gledge End and turned off it to by-roads and then stooged around.'

'What was the number of your bike, sir?'

'Number? Oh, I don't remember. It was a red and silver affair, a Kotsac, very unreliable.'

'From whom did you hire it?'

'That garage in Long Cove Bay just as you enter the town. May I ask what all this is in aid of?'

'Did you meet anybody while you were out, sir?'

'Not to say *meet* anybody. I picked up a girl at the pub and took her on the pillion.'

'Her name, sir?'

'Marion was all I got, no surname. If she's in any trouble I can't help you. Nothing happened while we were out except that the beastly bike broke down and the garage chap couldn't see to it immediately, so by the time it was tuned up — there was nothing much wrong — Marion had got sick of waiting and I suppose she went home on the bus. I couldn't blame her.'

'Did you pass a girl cyclist on the moor, sir?'

'No. We passed a couple of hikers, but they were both men. Oh, later on I saw another fellow. He was stooping over a buckled bike. I shouldn't think it was his own, though. Looked like a lady's machine to me. The front wheel seemed to have taken a bit of a knock. He was trying to straighten it, I think, but I didn't stop and I don't think Marion even noticed.'

'Where was this, sir?'

'Good Lord! I don't know. I was just out for a ride. Oh, half a minute, though. I do know more or less where it was. I had just passed a signpost to Wayland.'

'Can you describe the man? How was he dressed?'

'I only saw him as I whizzed by, and only his back view, anyway. I believe I remember a rucksack, but I couldn't speak to anything else.'

'You saw a buckled bike, probably a lady's machine, and this man bending over it. Nothing else?'

'Nothing else. I mean, there was nobody who looked as though she might have had an accident, otherwise I would have stopped.'

'I see, sir. Thank you for your help. May I have your home

address in case I need to be in touch with you again?'

It was not far from the farm to the Bull and on the way Ribble, who was thorough-going, first pulled up at the garage which Adam Penshaw had mentioned and checked on the hiring of motorcycles. They recognised his description of the young man and showed him the red and silver Kotsac. They kept self-drive cars for the hire of summer visitors to the resort and a couple of motorcycles, 'although there's not much call for them, especially at this time of year, Inspector.'

Ribble took down the registration number of the Kotsac and drove into the town. The Bull was in the middle of its Friday-night revels and the place was full, the dartboard besieged and the pin-tables in full and noisy occupation. Among the customers Ribble recognised some of the party from the Youth Hostel. Apparently they had given up serious rehearsal in favour of conviviality, which did not argue any lasting concern for the dead girl.

The scene was lively and the bar was crowded and very busy. It was hardly the best time to make enquiries, but Ribble wanted to press on. It did not seem to him that he had made much progress so far. Checking the activities of Giles and Plum at the church hall and Peggy's hairdressing appointment would have to wait until the morning and, in any case, he expected little to come from either. His chief hope was to gain further knowledge of the man who had inspected the buckled bicycle. The girl Marion might have noticed something which had escaped Adam Penshaw. The trouble might be to trace her, which was his reason for going to the pub. Ribble had little doubt that the bicycle had been the property of the dead woman. The turning to Wayland which Adam had mentioned seemed to prove it.

The bar was being attended to by a man and woman. Ribble waited until he could order his beer from the latter. When he received his pint from her he asked whether she knew a girl named Marion.

'She was in here yesterday between twelve and one with a young fellow named Penshaw,' he said. 'Looks about eighteen.'

'Oh yes? I don't recollect the name,' she said. 'What's this about Marion? Of course I know her. She's always in here. Picks up fellows and gets a lot of free drinks that way. I don't think she picked up your fellow, though. She wouldn't reckon on a lad of that age having enough money to treat her in the way she was accustomed, and she's never one to waste her time.'

'Would you know her address?'

'Sorry. Any way, I'm wanted.' A customer at the other end of the bar was becoming insistent. 'If you want her she'll be in here tomorrow at her usual time. Hang on! That's her just coming in. The girl in the cherry-coloured trousers.'

Ribble made his way over. The girl was unaccompanied, he was glad to see. In passing her as she made tracks for the bar, he jostled her and turned with a courteous apology.

'All right,' she said. 'No harm done. You've spilt your drink, though.'

'Not on you, miss, I'm relieved to notice. Perhaps you would do me the honour?'

'Oh, well, I don't mind if I do. Help to heal my bruises, won't it?'

They made their way to the dispensers of refreshment, Ribble this time getting the barman to serve him, and then found a vacant table in a far corner. Conversation of a light-hearted nature followed and then Ribble bought another round of drinks.

'How did you get on with young Penshaw yesterday?' he asked. 'He told me about you and how you went out on the back of his motorbike. Did you have a good time?'

'Depends what you call a good time. The blessed bike broke down. At least, he said it did.'

'Oh?'

'And he had no right to take a girl out and leave her kicking her heels in a rotten little public park in Gledge End while he went off to get the thing fixed. I did think a gentleman would have given a girl some lunch in a hotel and left me in the lounge with some magazines or something. Do you know he was gone for a good hour and a half! And it not being the time of year for a girl to sit out in a public park kicking her heels while a fellow gets a motorbike mended, well, I stayed there the hour and a half, like I said, it not being my way to stand a fellow up, but then I got cold and fed-up and went to the bus stop and got on the bus. I didn't know how long it might take to get the bike mended, not knowing what had gone wrong with it, and I hadn't had no proper lunch or me tea, so I reckoned I was justified not waiting about. I come in here last night and midday today thinking I'd see him, but nothing doing. Perhaps he thought I might give him a piece of my mind, keeping a girl hanging about like that, but I'm not that sort and I will say for him that he was good company and proper larky.'

'So you haven't seen him again,' said Ribble. 'Well, I've got to get back. Can I drop you anywhere?'

'Oh, well, p'raps you can, then, but I'm a respectable girl, you know. Thanks for the drinks; but it's one kiss on the doorstep and no admission to the old bedsitter.'

Ribble drove her home under her directions and, possibly to her disappointment, offered no kiss on the doorsteps. He now had her address if he needed it, although he did not think she could help him.

# —9—

# ACRID LOBELIA

Ribble's Saturday began with another visit to Mrs Beck's cottage. So far the only address he had taken down was that of the dead woman, Judy Tyne. As his next port of call was to be the hairdresser visited (according to her account) by Peggy, he needed her surname too, and thought he had better check the rest of the addresses as well.

Mrs Beck went over to the hostel and returned with the cards which the troupe had previously handed in. Although they had not taken their departure, they were not staying another night. Ribble sat down and wrote busily, adding the home addresses to the names of Giles Tranmire, Willie Nicolson, Peter Hutton, Plum (Pelham) Redman, Mick (Michael) Mardon, Ronald Brawby, Peggy (Margaret) Raincliffe and Pippa (Philippa) Mardon, Mick's sister.

At the hairdresser's, as he had other calls to make and time was pressing, he produced the evidence of his official standing to an enquiring young person at the appointments desk and asked her to verify that 'a Miss Raincliffe had booked a hair-do lasting about an hour on last Thursday morning, if you will be so good, miss.'

The girl said that she would have to ask. She went to a tall woman who was doing complicated things involving clips and rollers and murmured to her. Ribble heard her say: 'He'll have to wait until I get Mrs, Rollins under the drier.'

Ribble walked over to them.

'I am investigating a serious accident,' he said. 'All I want to know is at what time this customer, Miss Raincliffe, came in here on Thursday and at what time she left. It only means looking her up in your book.'

'Very well, if that's all,' said the tall woman. 'Nothing to do with a complaint, I hope.'

'Unless you call death a complaint,' said Ribble, taking the receptionist back to the desk. 'Now, miss, if you would kindly turn back to Thursday, Raincliffe is the name I'm looking for.'

'I'll check, but I don't remember it. No, it's not down in the bookings.'

'What about Wednesday?'

'No, not Wednesday neither.'

'You haven't turned back to Wednesday, miss.'

The girl flipped back a page in the ledger. A line was drawn diagonally across the sheet.

'On account we're closed Wednesday because we're open all day Saturday,' she explained.

'Well, concerning Thursday, is it possible for ladies to get a hair-do without booking beforehand?'

'If it was only a trim we might be able to fit a person in, or if there was a cancellation, not otherwise.'

¬ 'Do you remember anybody dropping in like that on Thursday?'

'I'm sure nobody did.'

'Have you an assistant here named Marcelle?'

'Marcia, not Marcelle.'

'Point her out to me, please.'

'She don't do hair, she only washes it, not being full-trained. She's at the far basin. You better wait till she's done the second shampoo and rinse.'

Ribble had no time for these niceties. He walked over to the hair-washer and said, 'No need to stop what you're doing. Did you have a client named Raincliffe at about midday on Thursday?'

The girl suspended operations, but only for a second.
'Nope,' she said, and went on with her job.
'Are you absolutely certain?'
'Yup.'
'Is there another assistant with a name something like yours?'
At this point the woman who appeared to be in charge came up to them and said briskly, 'Mrs Rollins is under the drier. What can I do for you?' She led the inspector back to the desk.

'I am trying to trace the movements of a lady named Raincliffe,' he said in official tones, 'and the operative day is last Thursday, the time probably between twelve and one. This lady may have come without having made an appointment.'

'Most unlikely and, last Thursday, quite impossible.' She drew the appointments book towards her. 'We were fully booked and there were no cancellations.'

'You fitted in a trim, perhaps?'

'We are seldom able to do that, and certainly did not on Thursday.'

'Are there other ladies' hairdressers in the town?'

'There is an establishment in Dale Street, but the class of client who come here would hardly patronise it.'

Ribble thanked her, sought out the 'establishment in Dale Street' and drew another blank when he repeated his questions.

'Only Antoine's,' said the receptionist. 'Not that there is an Antoine, or ever will be. It belongs to the manageress. I suppose she thinks a man's name, and Frenchified at that, sounds better, but she isn't above pinching my best assistants when I've trained them. The tips are better there, you see, because of all the councillors' wives. I suppose they get their hair done out of the rates. You never know how many fiddles go on when it's rate-payers' money they're spending. A Miss Raincliffe? We have never had a client of that name.'

'I always go there,' quoted Ribble to himself, referring to Peggy's statement regarding Antoine's. It had been a stupid, witless lie. Obviously Antoine's had never heard of Peggy Raincliffe and, in any case, the shop was miles and miles from Peggy's home address. The girl must have had some reason for lying.

Besides, if she had not cycled to the hairdresser's and back during what must have been the time of Judy Tyne's death, where *had* she been, and why did it need to remain a secret?

He drove back to the hostel but, as he had anticipated, by the time he got there the troupe had collected their belongings and their cards and gone. Application to Mrs Beck resulted in the information that, so far as she knew, the dancers and musicians were over at Gledge End for a morning's rehearsal in the church hall before they gave their afternoon performance at three.

There were other things he could do before he made contact with Peggy Raincliffe. There were the men's movements to check. He thought at first that it would be of no use to go to the cinema at that time of day, but then he remembered that on Saturday mornings cinemas often opened to project a special programme for children. He expected little to come of his errand. It was most unlikely that the girl in the box-office would have any recollection of selling tickets to Willie and Mick, let alone having noted the times of their arrival and departure; nevertheless, as a conscientious police officer, he felt bound to make the enquiry.

He was right about the children's matinée, and wrong about the memory of the girl in the box-office. Yes, this was the only cinema in the place. Thursday afternoon? Well, it was only pensioners mostly, wasn't it? Sure she remembered two young men coming in. Describe them? She couldn't say as to that. They had come in as soon as the commissionaire opened the doors. First in the queue she reckoned they were. One was sort of tallish and dark and the other, well, really more like a girl until he spoke. Lovely silky blond hair and, well, lots of girls wore trousers and sweaters nowadays, didn't they?

She had fixed the time of their arrival, but about the time of their departure she was unhelpful. People came and went. Oh, yes, she had to stay on duty, the picture being continuous and people coming in at any old time. If she had been issuing tickets when the young men left she would not have noticed them go out, and, besides that, although there was only one entrance, there were other exits.

'Have to be. Suppose there was a fire?' she said impressively.

'You don't want panic, do you?'

Ribble tried the commissionaire.

'My job is to control the queue, if any,' said that official. 'Yes, I remember the two young fellows because they went in soon as I opened the doors. See 'em leave? Not as I recollect. I daresay they used one of the other exits. Besides, they might not have exited together. They *came* together, oh, yes, certainly they did, but that's not to say they exited together. Young chaps don't always have the same fish to fry, do 'em? Mind you, when I first seen 'em I thought they was two of a kind, if you take my meaning, so perhaps they did leave together, but I wouldn't know, would I, being solicitous in my dooty and earning my money non-union, which is to say without benefit of shop steward.'

The idea that, before the end of the programme, the two young men might have separated had already occurred to Ribble. If Mick really had fallen asleep, there could have been nothing to prevent Willie from slipping out. The question was whether he had been able to slip back to wake Mick up and take him and the tandem back to the hostel. The inspector applied again to the box-office.

'Look,' said the girl somewhat austerely, 'are you a debt-collector or something?'

'I am a police officer. I only want to know whether either of the young men you described asked for re-admission, having left the cinema either by the main entrance or one of the exits early on. He couldn't get back in again through one of the emergency exits, could he?'

'If he could, I should be out of a job, because if *he* could, so could everybody else, couldn't they?'

'Ask a silly question!' thought Ribble. He thanked the girl and drove to the swimming pool. Here he was no luckier. Thursday, the girl at the *guichet* reminded him, was early-closing day in the town. What with that, and the schools being on half-term holiday, the pool had been so well patronised that it was impossible for her to remember any particular customers.

'These would be strangers to you,' Ribble pointed out,' so I thought perhaps you might have noticed them.' However, she remained firm. The only people she was at all likely to remember, she said, were those who hired towels and that happened very seldom and had not happened on Thursday. As for strangers, what did he expect in a holiday town? There were *always* strangers coming along for a swim.

'You would hardly swim in the sea this time of year,' she reminded him,' so, of course, they come here.'

'In October?'

'Well, not so much as in the summer, but, like I said, we get a lot of custom. Why not,' she concluded, 'when we've got a nice clean heated pool so handy, and diving boards and a chute and showers and everything.'

Ribble agreed and reflected that blest were they who expected nothing, for they could not be disappointed. He went back to his car and drove to the church hall. Here a man with a wheelbarrow was tidying up the churchyard which was adjacent to the ground on which the hall had been built. Ribble asked where he could find the caretaker of the hall.

'That's me,' said the man, 'but the churchwardens does the lettings. Their addresses is on the board.'

'I am a police officer.'

'We're fully licensed and the fire regulations is adhered to.'

'Last Thursday — Thursday of this week — two young fellows came to arrange the chairs for a show which is to be put on in the church hall this afternoon. How would they have got admission to the hall to do that?'

'Same as any other hirers get in. My name and address is on the notice-board too, and they had the key off of me, having produced their letter which the churchwardens had signed up. Everything was in order, you can bet on it.'

'So you saw and spoke with them. Are they here now?'

'I reckon the whole lot's here. There's eight of 'em been at it all the time, a fiddle and a penny whistle and sometimes the piano thumping out, and tapping with their sticks and jingling the little bells on their trouser-legs and thudding on the floor with their hopping and jumping and giving a sort of a shout every now and again, you never heard such a racket. I peeped in once or twice and they was always hard at it 'cepting when they knocked off to have an argy-bargy about what somebody was doing wrong. They're arguing now, I reckon. There don't seem to be no music nor stamping nor jingling nor nothing. Come on in, if you want to see 'em.'

They found the company resting their legs but not their tongues. A lively discussion was going on.

'I tell you,' said Pippa, 'that my flute is perfectly adequate for the hornpipe. I know we used to have your violin, but that's beside the point now, because you're wanted for the dance in Judy's place.'

'The flute sounds silly for the hornpipe,' said Peggy. 'Failing Judy's concertina, the fiddle is the only thing. Whoever heard of a hornpipe being danced to the flute?'

'Well, somebody can play the piano, then,' said Willie.

'Oh, no, they can't' said Giles. 'It would be a complete anachronism or worse. Whoever heard of deck-hands dancing to a piano.? It would be better to have three men dance the hornpipe and let Peggy fiddle for us, only unfortunately that can't be done, unless Mick will do it as a girl. The tiny little shorts and middy blouse that Judy used to wear would look ridiculous on anyone else and we simply haven't got another pair of bell-bottoms for a man to wear.'

'I can't get into Judy's rig, as you know very well,' snapped Peggy, 'so, unless Mick will do it, that's that.'

'You've got navy shorts of your own and I can lend you a white sweater. The audience *likes* having a girl in the middle. Actually the rather rakish cap is the only thing that really matters, apart from the girl's legs, and you've got very nice legs, Peggy. I've often noticed them,' said Giles.

'Oh, you have, have you?'

'Going back to the flute,' said Pippa, 'I don't want to start an argument, but actually the hornpipe wasn't originally a dance at all. It was a musical instrument, one of the ancestors of the oboe. It was a pipe with holes at the mouth end and a real cow's horn at the bell-end, so you see a flute would really be much more in keeping than a fiddle, anyway, as I've always pointed out.'

'The sailors always danced to the fiddle. It's traditional,' said Peggy. 'Anyway, I am not going to wear navy shorts and Giles's white sweater. Besides, the hornpipe is really a solo dance. Think of Wayne Sleep.'

'All right, all right,' said Giles, 'but we haven't got a Wayne Sleep, so there will be three of us doing the hornpipe as usual. Peggy will play for it and Mick will dance the girl in the middle.'

'Not in Judy's shorts he won't said Mick. 'I've got hairy legs. I'm all right in *Three Meet* because I'm wearing a frock and white stockings, but the hornpipe? Why can't just the two of you do it?'

At this point, Ribble thought that unless he intervened the argument was likely to go on for some time.

'Excuse me,' he said, 'I shan't keep you more than a moment. Just checking.' He turned to the caretaker. 'Well?'

'Him and him,' said the caretaker, pointing to Giles and Plum.

'Right.' He looked at the rows of chairs. 'At what time did they hand back the keys to you?'

'They never. They dropped them through my letter-box.'

Ribble dismissed him and addressed the company. 'I am continuing my investigations into the death of Mrs Tyne. Does anybody want to change his story of how he spent Thursday afternoon? I've already found one discrepancy,' he said austerely.

'I don't know why you're looking at me,' said Peggy.

'No, miss? I would be glad to inform you if we could have a word in private.'

'Oh, I say!' exclaimed Giles. 'Our rehearsal, you know.'

Ribble took Peggy out into the vestibule.

'You lied to me, miss,' he said flatly.

'Suppose I did?'

'It's a serious matter, miss. I am investigating the circumstances of violent death. For your own sake it would be better to confide in me. You are known to have quarrelled with the deceased.'

'I don't like being threatened.'

'That is not a threat, miss, just a friendly warning.'

'Well, if you must know, I went to Crosswell.'

'A good deal of time would have been saved if you had told me that at once, miss.'

'You didn't think I would confess to chasing after a boy, did you? Anyway, I didn't catch up with him — Mick I'm talking about. I knew he had gone off with Willie. I had heard their plans and with Judy out of the way — of course I didn't know what was happening to her — I went after them, but they can kick that tandem along so fast that they had left the restaurant in Crosswell by the time I got to it, and I didn't know they had gone to the pictures. I looked round the shops and then cycled back, that's all.'

'What time was this, miss?'

'I suppose I left Crosswell soon after three and I pedalled back pretty hard. I was upset at not catching Mick, you see.'

Ribble had a good deal to think about. As Peggy had lied once, she might be lying again. As for Mick, he claimed to have fallen asleep in the cinema, but what if, with or without Willie's connivance, he had slipped out when the lights went down, met Peggy by arrangement and that together they had tracked Judy down and murdered her?

He could see the snags in this theory. It was most unlikely that they would have known what Judy's plans were when she left the hostel. All the same, she might have confided them to Mick, owing to her special feeling for him. The difficulty was the time factor. The killing had to be done in a lonely part of the countryside and, unless Judy had made a previous assignation with Mick, it would have been simply a matter of luck whether he and his accomplice Peggy came upon Judy in the lonely spot where the body had been found.

In any case, there were still questions to be asked. Had Judy become so much of a nuisance to Mick that he was prepared to go so far as to kill her? Ribble doubted it. Then there was Willie to consider. Had Mick really fallen asleep in the cinema and had Willie been the one to slip out? But there was no evidence whatever that either of the boys had left the cinema during the performance, and they must have come back to the hostel together because their means of transport was the tandem.

Ribble abandoned these speculations for another. There was no reason, on the face of it, to suspect either Giles or Plum, but although they could find a witness, the caretaker, to the time they had arrived at the church hall to arrange the seating, there was no proof of the time at which they had left, since they had not handed back the keys, but had put them throught the caretaker's letter-box. It seemed unlikely that Giles would have been a party to the murder of one of his troupe, particularly just before one of their shows, but anger often over-rides expediency.

Ribble sighed. It seemed that he could rule out nobody but Mick's sister Pippa. Even the two who had gone to the swimming pool must remain suspect. He reverted to Mick and Willie. The tandem need not have had two passengers on the journey back from Crosswell. Either of the young men could have pedalled it back (with a wobble or two because of its length) and the other could have come back on the bus. There were bus routes into Long Cove Bay to connect it with other towns and the outlying villages and there could have been an arrangement whereby the boys met at the Long Cove Bay bus terminus in order to come back on the tandem to the hostel as though they had been together all the time.

Unfortunately, although he felt certain that one or more of the members of Wild Thyme could be held responsible for Judy Tyne's death, he had not ruled out the possibility that some hit-and-run motorist had knocked her off her bicycle — how else to account for that buckled front wheel? — and, to save himself from being reported by the girl to the police, had decided to finish her off and try to hide the body.

The last possibility was that the escaped convict, desperate for money and food, had been the murderer. Ribble had almost, but not quite, rejected this theory, but while the man was still at large, no theory could be abandoned completely.

Mentally Ribble tossed up. Heads the murderer was Willie, for the Yorkshireman did not trust the dark Celt. Willie might have had every incentive to remove one of Mick's lovers. If he had done so, the girl Peggy might also be in danger. Tails, the murderer was Mick himself. Ribble had the usual masculine distrust of fair-haired, girlish-looking boys, especially when they were under such close protection as that of the saturnine Willie.

Ribble sighed again. Peggy herself, as he had already realised, must remain on the list of suspects. She had already lied about her movements and even if she had told the truth now, there were hours of Thursday for which she could provide only the most sketchy of accounts.

# —10—

# WILD THYME (2)

The rehearsal over, the dancers sat on the rather uncomfortable chairs and put their stockinged feet up while Peggy and Pippa were sent out by Giles to the shops in Gledge End to purchase food and soft drinks for the party. The meal was to be taken in the church hall to save time and conserve energy.

'Take the tandem,' said Willie handsomely. 'If you hitch the trailer you can bring back lots of grub and plenty to drink. Your little handlebar baskets won't hold nearly enough for all of us.'

'Not too much liquid,' said Giles, the leader. 'When it's over we'll go to the pub, but we don't want a lot of fizz sloshing about inside us before we dance.'

The platform in the hall, dignified, when the building was hired, by being called the stage, was on this occasion to be used to seat some of those who had bought the most expensive tickets. On one side of it there was an entrance through a doorway in the back wall to a room in which, on Sundays, a class for the youngest Sunday School children could be held, and when the hall was let on weekdays the room served as a changing-room and had a washroom attached to it. It also contained a very roomy cupboard for the caretaker's brooms and buckets.

After the indoor picnic-style lunch the company rested while Pippa practised an obbligato she was to play with an orchestra in a concert in her own town and Giles knit his brows over the afternoon programme and hoped that Mick would be able to cope with the extra rôles assigned to him in place of Judy. The show was to open at three and was to begin with a set of three folk-songs sung by the whole company including the violinist. The plump Peggy was to wear a print dress and a sunbonnet and at Giles's orders, although against her own wishes, Pippa was to be disguised in a beard and false eyebrows. These were in the property box, but seldom used except for the more bucolic of the folk-songs, when they were worn by Plum. Pippa had done her best to repudiate them, but Giles was adamant.

'As Mick looks so much like you now he is dressed as a girl for the hornpipe and Three Meet and Parson's Farewell,' he said, agreement having been reached that Mick would take the girl's part in these dances, with Peggy as the other girl in Parson's Farewell, 'we simply must iron out the resemblance, don't you see, dear?'

'It's very unorthodox,' said Peggy, 'to have Mick in the hornpipe as a sort of bumboat woman.'

'Well, it makes it more fun,' said Giles. 'I still don't see why a white sweater and your navy shorts, with the sailor cap and your bare feet, wouldn't do for you, but there you are. You insist on playing your fiddle for it. And Mick, you dance it straight. If you go putting on an *ad lib* and ogling the two sailors, the audience will know you're a man, and that may get you a laugh, but it will utterly ruin Three Meet, so no capers, if you please. Save them for the Morris where they belong.'

'In name, if not in nature,' said Plum.

'I wonder why the things you pickle are also called capers?' said Peter, who thought the conversation was becoming charged with nervous tension.

'The vegetable kind are named after a Middle English word, *caperes*,' said Giles. 'The movements called capers in a dance are a sort of bowdlerised version of *capriole*, which I imagine is French.'

'Oh, yes, there's Peter Warlock's *Capriole Suite*. You ought to make up some dances to that music, Giles. I believe the Rambert Ballet used to do that, or so my oldest aunt told me. She saw them at the old Lyric Theatre in Hammersmith,' said Ronnie, backing up Peter's effort to calm the party.

'There is another use for the word 'caper' which is not so generally known,' said Willie. 'There is a Manx proverb which says, "The weather is so foul that not even a caper will venture out." In this connection a caper was an Irish fisherman from Cape Clear. These chaps had the reputation for venturing out to sea in any weather.'

'Join Wild Thyme and get yourself a liberal education,' said Giles. 'Well, I think it's time we got changed. If I mistake not, our audience will soon be arriving.'

It had been arranged that the caretaker would be 'on the door' to tear the tickets and that Peggy would show people to their seats as, for her, there would be no costume changes. The caretaker had strict instructions to let no latecomers in during a dance, but to allow them to find their seats (without Peggy's assistance) if they arrived while nothing but a feast of song was being offered. All the songs were sung in unison as choruses. There were no vocal soloists. In any case, very few late arrivals were anticipated. As Peter put it: 'We who live north of a line drawn from Stafford to Kings Lynn are jolly well going to see the *whole* of a performance for which we've shelled out our brass.'

'Are you going to act on that tip the forestry warden gave you?' Peggy enquired of Giles, while the company still kept their seats.

'Worth trying, I think,' he said. 'It won't be much fun pedalling our bikes forty miles to the next Youth Hostel after we've done the show, and the last twenty miles will be after dark. If I can get you two girls fixed up for the night it will be something. We chaps must take our chance. I'd like to get Mick a bed near here, as he's got such an extra load of dancing to do now that we haven't Judy with us, but that would involve Willie, because of the tandem. Oh, well, we'll see what the response is from the forest cabins. I know there are one or two empty cabins at this time of year, but I suppose it would be against regulations for the warden to let us have a couple of those for the night, even at a reasonable fee which we could easily afford out of the ticket money.'

'Well, I hope something comes up for us,' said Peggy, 'and for you boys, too. A few miles to the forest is a vastly different proposition from forty miles to the next hostel and some of it after dark. It wasn't even dark when Judy was pulled off her bike.'

'We don't know that she was pulled off it,' said Giles, 'so don't start all that up again. We've got the show to think about.' He was feeling his responsibilities acutely. There had been all too little time to rehearse the changes in the programme which had been made necessary by Judy's absence, and there had even been serious discussion of a suggestion by Pippa that the most spectacular item should be left out altogether. This was their own version of the traditional sword dance called Kirkby Malzeard and titled by Giles, who had imposed a dramatically bloody ending on it, Ritual Slaughter at Kirkby Moorside.

'We can't do it properly with seven people, even if I do the hobby horse,' she said, 'and Peggy can't dance in it because you say we must have her for the music, but I still can't see why my flute wouldn't do. Peggy would do the hobby horse better than I shall.'

'We settled all that,' said Giles, 'and I've spent a lot of time coaching you.'

'I know, but I'm still nervous about how I shall perform.'

'It isn't as though you have to dance,' said Giles. 'So long as you keep out of the dancers' way and only make little dashes at the audience and flick the horse's tail in their faces and cavort about a bit, you'll do fine. And Peter made the head and the rest of the gear very light because Judy was going to wear it, so you know you can support it all right. We know it's really a man's part, but you'll manage.'

Pippa began to cry.

'I think it's in dreadfully bad taste to dance a ritual killing when we know what's happened to Judy,' she said.

'Oh, stop beefing!' said Plum. 'No need to bring that up.'

'On another matter,' said Giles, 'I've notified the local press and I expect they'll take photographs after the show, so nobody is to change out of costume until they've done with us.'

'I'm not going to be photographed wearing that awful contraption you call the hobby horse's head,' said Pippa, still in tears.

'All right, all right. You'll still be wearing your beard, so you can take off the head, but be sure you hold it in profile. It's Peter's *pièce de rèsistance* and I want it to stand out.'

'I don't want to be photographed in the beard, either.'

'Look, I've explained about the beard. You and Mick *must* be differentiated.'

'But *he* wears a beard for the Morris and the sword dances.'

'Quite a different beard, and I've trimmed yours so that you can find your lips for your flute. What's the matter with you, Pippa? It isn't like you to kick up this sort of damn silly fuss.'

'If you want to know, I'm scared. Judy was murdered — you know she was. And if Mick plays the victim he'll be murdered, too. I don't want to stay the night in one of the forest cabins, either. It's not safe. As soon as the show is over I am getting on my bike and going home.'

The show was scheduled to last for an hour and a half. There were only two items which would not be repeated for an encore. Whether the audience called for encores or not was beside the point, Giles pointed out. The time had to be filled in somehow, or people would not feel they were getting their money's worth. The exceptions were the four groups of folk-songs ('they wouldn't get an encore, anyway — we don't sing well enough') and the Ritual Murder dance with which the programme ended.

'We may be offering a rather truncated version of what I originally planned,' said Giles, 'but even that would lose all its drama if we repeated it. That bloody head is another masterpiece of Peter's. We end on that and I don't expect much applause for any other item. People in these parts only really like vulgar comedians and audience participation in the songs, and they'll be highly critical of our old-style folk-songs and dances and, of course, they do like a full orchestra which makes plenty of lively noise, not just a violin and a flute with occasional piano accompaniment.'

'Oh, don't encourage us, whatever you do,' said Peggy bitterly. 'As though we don't already feel inadequate enough!'

'Oh, quite a few of the forest cabin people are coming,' said
Ronnie soothingly. 'They'll appreciate us, I'm sure, and we are
not repeating any of the songs unless they applaud them quite
wildly — and they won't.'

'We had better get changed,' said Giles. 'Good luck, everybody.'

'We shall need it,' said Peter. The programme opened with
three of the songs. All the songs, of which there were a round
dozen, were arranged in groups of three and in all of them Judy's
clear soprano was sorely missed, although Peter could manage a
passable counter-tenor and Mick what the others called 'a Hinge-
and-Bracket' voice. Pippa did not sing, her lips being otherwise
engaged, but Peggy, at the piano for the songs, had a robust con-
tralto and Plum contributed a resounding bass.

As the first three songs were to be followed by the folk dances
called Three Meet and Parsons Farewell, Mick was able to appear
in his girl-rig for the opening choruses, so that he had no need of a
costume change for the first two dances. The other men were in
the white flannel trousers which they would also wear for the
morris and sword dances,but would be without their ribbon-
streamer hats and the bells on their legs. While any changes of
costume were being made in the little room behind the platform,
the two girls were to play the flute and violin solos taking it in
turns to accompany one another on the piano, and there would
also be a rendering of various sentimental airs known, it was
hoped, to most of the audience.

'The tickets are not numbered,' said Erica, 'so we had better get
there in good time if we want to find a good seat. I'm surprised
that a church hall has a stage big enough for dancing.'

'It will probably be staged at floor level,' said the knowledgeable Isobel. 'When these sort of people come to give a performance at my school, they use the body of the hall and the kids sit
around on all four sides, leaving a big space in the middle. I expect
that's what it will be like this afternoon.'

The church hall had its carpark and only half-a-dozen cars
were in it when they arrived. Peggy, at her most gracious, her

generous body encased in a small black velvet bolero and a very full flowered skirt topped by a white muslin blouse, was also wearing white stockings and shining black shoes. She asked whether they would like seats on the platform — 'you can have four in the middle of the front row' — or whether they would prefer to be in the body of the hall and, receiving an answer, took them on to the small stage.

The choice had been made by Tamsin, who immediately saw that John Trent was up there. She appropriated the chair next to his at the end of the front row.

'We thought you had gone home,' she said.

'No,' he said. 'We had to get out of our cabin before ten this morning, so we left soon after breakfast and I took my parents home and came back here, but I'm afraid I can't stay to the end.'

'We didn't think we should see you again.'

'Oh, these bad pennies, you know. Hullo, isn't that your clinging vine in the doorway?'

'Oh, dear, yes. We hoped he had moved on.'

'It doesn't look like it, and he is headed this way. He's got two people with him.'

Adam, who was coming towards the platform, was waylaid by Peggy. They heard her say: 'Sorry, but your ticket doesn't entitle you to sit up there. This way, please.' The middle-aged couple who had accompanied him were already being directed by the caretaker to the second row down below. Adam shrugged his shoulders and took a seat in the body of the hall as near to the door as he could get, and the couple got up and joined him, but, a few words having been exchanged, they returned to the more central seats in the second row to which they had first been directed, and the bulk of the audience began to come in.

Like many amateur performances, the show started late, Mick having mislaid a shoe, but by twenty minutes past three the two musicians had taken their places and soon the company was rendering the first of three folk-songs with Pippa at the piano, her flute in its case resting on the chair next to Peggy, who was accompanying on the violin.

The audience was not a large one, although a certain amount of money had been taken at the door, but the applause was more generous than Giles had expected it to be. The songs went down well, the dances even better, and it was a flushed and happy company which gathered in the dressing-room at the end of the dance in which Mick had been ritually slain and the bloody head carried round in triumph, a considerable alteration to the original version, but one well received by the audience.

John Trent, among others, missed this grand finale and Adam Penshaw saw even less of the show than John, for he stayed only for the three opening songs and the two folk-dances which followed them. John stayed until four o'clock and then took advantage of his place at the end of the row near the platform steps, which he had chosen so that he could slip away without disturbing anybody, gave Tamsin's hand a squeeze and made an unobtrusive exit in the middle of three sea-shanties which preceded the hornpipe. The songs were to give Mick time to take off the beard he wore as a morris and sword dancer (different in colour and shape from the one which Pippa so much disliked on herself) and get into the blonde wig, black stockings and a skirt borrowed from Peggy, ready to dance as a bumbboat woman between Giles and Plum, the two sailors. The choruses were left therefore to the depleted choir consisting of Peter, Ronnie, Willie and Peggy, with Pippa, also singing, at the piano.

Under cover of the sea-shanties Tamsin murmured to Hermione, who was seated between her and Isobel, 'John asked for my address.'

'Did you give it to him?'

'Yes. he said he would write.'

'Pity he has to go home.'

As soon as the performance was over and the audience were beginning to leave the hall, the performers, pleased with themselves, remained in the dressing-room while the audience was dispersing. The hall being clear except for the chairs and a certain amount of litter, the caretaker came round to say that the photographer was ready. Giles went out to speak to him and learned that he wanted to take several pictures from which the editor of the local paper would make a selection.

As the company, including Pippa as the hobby horse, were still in their sword-dance costumes, that group was taken first and was to be followed by the folk-dancers. This involved only four of the company: Giles, Willie, Peggy, and Mick in his impersonation of a girl. The first three had little alteration to make in their costumes, but it was different for Mick.

'I'll be a minute or two getting my beard off and myself into the petticoats,' he said. 'Tell the chap I'll be as quick as I can.'

'Well, while you're changing, the rest of us can begin clearing the hall. It's wanted for the Youth Club tonight and the caretaker has to get the floor and the platform swept and the table-tennis trestles and boards out. I promised we would stack up the chairs and move the piano to where he wants it, so we can save a bit of our own time if we start the chores now. The photographer will have to wait,' said Giles.

This business of changing his clothes took Mick so long, apparently, that when all the chairs were stacked, the platform cleared and the piano moved, he still had not joined the others.

'He must have stuck too much glue on that beard, or something,' said the photographer, who was becoming restless. 'Could one of you go and hurry him up a bit? I've got another assignment to cover.'

'I'll go,' said Peggy immediately. She darted away before anyone else could offer to go, and banged the heavy door shut behind her. Ten more minutes went by and the photographer said that he proposed to make do with the pictures he had already taken, and promptly removed himself and his camera. Giles, who had bounded towards the dressing-room, returned to find him gone. He had news for his team.

'Not a sign of either of them,' he said. 'Mick must have got changed, because his girl-outfit has gone and his flannels and bells and things are on the floor in the little washroom. I can't think what has happened.'

'I can,' said Pippa and Willie in unison. They looked at one another and Willie continued, 'She was always after him. I reckon it was a put-up job between them. He is a weak, soft-hearted fellow, so she's had her own way at last and taken him off with her. She swore to Judy that she would have him all to herself one day, and I think she's proved herself right.'

'Well, some girls in one of the forest cabins have offered to take Pippa for the night,' said Giles to the others, 'but the rest of us have got to get to the next hostel and that's forty miles off. Be hanged to those two idiots! They'll have either the tandem or Peggy's own bike and one of ours. They must have slipped out by the back door. It was open when I went in.'

The bicycles had been left in an unlocked shed near the main door of the hall, so the party went out that way. The tandem was gone, but the trailer which held the properties was still there.

'We'll have to leave it here for a day or two,' said Giles to the caretaker. 'I'll get it picked up as soon as I can. Willie, you'll have to put up the saddle on Peggy's bike and ride that, I'm afraid. It's no good cursing. Come on, or we shall hardly make the hostel by ten and that's the deadline.'

'What's that on your shoe?' asked Peter. Giles glanced down and said, 'Looks as though I trod on a tube of red greasepaint in the changing-room. Somebody must have dropped it. Come on! Come on! Pippa, you know the way to the forest and they gave you the number of the cabin, didn't they? Be seeing you!'

'I want to go with you.'

'No, no. You be a good girl and go to that forest cabin for the night. They'll be expecting you. We shall be better on our own. We're going to scorch. You would never be able to keep up.'

'Oh, all right.' She mounted her bicycle, waved good-bye and cycled northwards to where Erica was preparing a hot supper for the four young women and the two visitors they expected, for Peggy had also been offered a bed in the cabin.

'I'm sorry for those boys,' Tamsin had said, 'but we're doing our bit, anyway.'

'Oh, who cares about boys?' retorted Isobel. 'They are simply little things which are sent to try us. You'd know, if you had them in school, as I have.'

'I have them on building-sites, and I'm inclined to agree with you,' said Erica.

'Fancy John turning up like that!' said Tamsin. 'I was awfully glad.'

'A marriage has been arranged and will shortly take place,' said Hermione. Tamsin picked up a lump of dough from Erica's pastryboard and flung it at her.

# $-11-$

# BLOOD-CAP

Innocent and ignorant of what had actually happened to Mick and Peggy, and attaching quite the wrong explanation to the wide-open back door which led out of their changing-room, Giles and the others pedalled away like racing cyclists, and as the caretaker had gone out with them to the shed, he had no idea that the back door, which he always kept bolted on the inside to frustrate mischievous boys, had been opened and left open. He saw the party off, and accepted their view that the missing pair had sneaked round to the bicycle shed, taken the tandem and gone off together. He went back by the main door into the hall.

Although the Wild Thyme party had stacked the chairs, moved the piano, cleared the platform and done their best to clear up the litter left by their audience — litter inseparable, apparently, from any place of entertainment, indoors or out, patronised by the British public — he still had his own sweeping and dusting to do, and his table-tennis trestles and boards to set up.

Thankful to see the last of the dancers, he pocketed the tip Giles had given him and went into the changing-room to get his broom and duster. These, with the rest of his cleaning materials, were kept in the deep, commodious cupboard which took up almost half of the wall-space next to the washroom. It was never kept locked. It was thought most unlikely that anyone would want to steal brooms and buckets or the Sunday School hymnbooks which were on a high shelf at the back.

The first thing he noticed was the open back door. He went over to close and bolt it, thinking (as Giles had thought) that the runaway couple had used it as their exit. When he reached it, however, he saw a stockinged foot protruding from one of the sooty, sour-looking bushes which formed part of the untended sideway.

He went over to investigate and thought at first that he was looking at a dead body. As he bent over it, however, it gave a faint groan. Then he noticed that it was wearing a heavy flaxen wig which had slipped partly over the face.

'It's the young chap that doubled as a girl,' he thought, for he had watched part of the rehearsal in which no time had been spent on costume-changes. The hall was not on the telephone, but one of the churchwardens lived close at hand. He raced over there to telephone for a doctor and the police. He was himself an expoliceman and some blood which had seeped into the flaxen wig convinced him that the youth had been attacked.

He made his telephone call and the churchwarden went back with him to the hall and suggested that they should carry Mick into the building.

'I wouldn't touch him, sir,' the caretaker replied, 'not until the doctor has seen him. Well, until he comes, I'd best get on. It's Youth Club night.'

Peggy's body fell forward out of the cupboard as he opened its unlocked door.

The doctor called an ambulance and Mick was taken to hospital. Ribble and Sergeant Nene turned up in time to see the boy carried off and then they turned their attention to the dead girl. The caretaker was allowed to get on with his chores, but was told not to leave until the police had questioned him. Meanwhile the doctor made his report, photographs and fingerprints were taken by the experts Ribble had brought with him and then the caretaker was questioned, although Ribble soon realised that the man could tell him little that was of much help.

Ribble knew him to have been a member of the Force and treated him accordingly.

'So you didn't expect to find the back door open,' he said.

'That I didn't, sir. Kids like to play in and out of those bushes, so I never give them the chance to sneak in. I don't know what's come over the youngsters nowadays. Don't seem happy unless they're wrecking something.'

'So one of the song-and-dance lot must have opened the door. I see that the bolts are all on the inside as usual.'

'Must have been one of them, sir, although it seems a bit strange, seeing that they used the room to change their costumes. Perhaps someone knocked and one of the party let him in.'

'Then that must have been the dead girl. The doctor thinks she was attacked from the front, whereas the boy who's been taken to hospital was almost certainly set upon from behind, like the girl on the moor. I suppose you don't know where the rest of the party were making for when they left here?'

'I know they talked about a Youth Hostel, sir, but I don't know where. I do know where one of them has gone, though. There was a short interval midway through the show and the young fellow who seems to be the leader asked whether any of the forest cabin people could offer a bed for the night to save the girls a long cycle ride, some of it after dark. A young lady sitting on the platform said her lot could take the two girls, but there were no offers to put up the boys.'

'Two girls? Oh, yes, this dead girl and the other one,'

'Name of Pippa, sir. She went off on her bicycle one way and the chaps went off in another direction. She wanted to go with them. It was thought, from what I gathered, that the other two had taken the tandem and sloped off together.'

'Oh, the tandem was missing, was it? Weren't the bikes locked up, then?'

'Well, sir, I thought they'd come to no harm. Some of the Youth Club come on bikes and motorbikes, so I always lock the shed door on Youth Club nights, but this afternoon the lock was only pushed together. It's just an ordinary padlock. I reckon the murderer opened up, pinched the tandem and rode off on it.'

'I'd better have a look at the shed. If there was only one man involved, somebody in the town must have seen him. Tandem bikes are not all that common, even with two people on them, and a chap riding one on his own would have been noticed, I should think. Of course there may have been two men involved.'

An inspection of the shed yielded nothing of importance. Ribble got his fingerprint expert busy on it, but the lock yielded no prints.

'Anybody pulling open a lock for the purpose of stealing a bike would know enough to have worn gloves or put a handkerchief over his hand,' said Sergeant Nene.

'Of course we don't know whether it was the murderer. Might have been an ordinary sneak-thief,' said Ribble, 'who spotted the bikes being put in and thought he would help himself to one of them. Bikes are valuable items nowadays.'

'I can tell you one thing, sir,' said the caretaker. 'The tandem wasn't gone until after about halfpast one. The young ladies came and rooted me out just as I finished my dinner (I only live just round the corner and had told them where my house was, just in case they needed anything as I could do for them before the show) and said they wanted to do some shopping for a picnic lunch in the hall. I told them the shed was unlocked and kept an eye open from my front window to watch for them coming back, and when I see them I come back and helped them with their shopping. I put the tandem away, and then I carried the stuff in as they'd bought, them helping me, and then I wheeled the trolley back through the hall for them and put it back in the shed so's they could load up their gear when the show was over, and that's how it was, sir.'

'When did the others miss this boy and girl?'

'The lad went to change into his frock and wig while the others were clearing the hall. He was gone for some time and the photographer from the local paper was getting cheesed off waiting, so the girl went to hurry the lad up. Then she never came back and the photographer wouldn't wait any longer. He had already got some pictures and he said he'd make those do. Then the others found the two were gone and so they said they would leave, too, and that's when they found as the tandem was missing and made it out as the two had gone off on it. Then I went to shut and bolt the back door and spotted the young fellow's foot sticking out of the bushes. That made me go off to telephone you and the doctor and then I opened up my broom cupboard and out tumbles that poor dead lass and then I see the blood on the floor, as I had not noticed previous.'

'And the other girl is staying the night in the forest, so she'll know where the rest of the party have gone. I shall have to see her, so that she can guide me to the others. Did you get the number of the forest cabin?'

'Yes, sir. I recollect as the young lady who made the offer mentioned cabin number eight.'

'Oh, good. As it happens, I know the occupants of that cabin, not that they'll be any too pleased to find me on their doorstep again. I can't think why you did not see the blood on the floor the minute you went in, though.'

'The window is very high up, sir, and my eyes were on the open door, which should have been shut, sir.'

Meanwhile, Pippa had covered most of her journey from the hall to the cabin when she picked up a puncture.

'That's *all* I needed!' she thought, as she pushed the bicycle the last half-mile down the forest track towards the cabins. 'Still, better here than on the road to the Youth Hostel. What on earth can have come over Mick to go off on the tandem with Peggy? He doesn't even like her. How did she manage to talk him into it?'

She pondered upon this question as she walked the useless bicycle past the beautiful forest trees, some still green, others in their glowing autumn colours. At any other time she would have delighted in her surroundings, but the puncture, the mysterious flight (as she still thought of it) of Peggy and Mick and the fact that the men in her party had gone off without her, combined to cloud her usually cheerful nature.

Isobel was waiting for her on the verandah.

'Hullo,' she said. 'Only one of you?'

'Yes, and I've got a puncture.'

'Oh, bad luck. Let's go round to the other door and then you can leave the bike in our little vestibule, where it will be under cover, and we'll help you mend the puncture if you've got the wherewithal in your little saddlebag. That was a first-class show you put on. We enjoyed it very much and so did the man we had with us.'

'Yes, your party on the platform led all the applause, and it made a lot of difference,' said Pippa, already feeling more cheerful. 'People always respond when anybody gives a lead. I've always noticed that.'

'The last item was a regular cliff-hanger. Where did you get that fearful-looking horse's head and the other one? That nearly turned us green because' — she had remembered the dead girl they had found on the moor and she changed what she had been about to say — 'because it looked so realistic.'

'Peter makes all our props. The hobby-horse thing I wore was his work, too,' said Pippa, as they wheeled the bicycle round the side of the cabin. 'He's an art student and awfully good at all that kind of thing.'

Inside the wooden building Erica was superintending her cooking and supper was soon on the table.

'I expect you're hungry after all that exertion,' she said. 'We loved the show.'

'We mostly give it to schools on Saturday mornings,' said Pippa, 'but this afternoon's may be the last one we shall do.'

'How's that?' asked Tamsin.

'We lost one of our members. That girl on the moor. And now my brother and the other girl have run away together.'

'Your brother? Which one was he?'

'He was the sacrificial victim in the last dance and he doubled as a girl in two of the folk-dances and the Irish jig and the hornpipe.'

'A man of parts indeed!' said Isobel.

'Tell us about the elopement. I didn't think such romantic doings happened nowadays,' said Erica.

'I don't think it was that kind of elopement,' said Pippa, scraping her plate. 'Peggy has been pursuing Mick for ages and I simply think she's got her hooks into him at last.'

'In other words, Europa has run off with the bull; but I have always thought it was that way round, you know. As I read the story, there was no reason for her to climb on the bull's back. Simply asking for trouble,' said Isobel.

'I expect the other girls dared Europa,' said Tamsin. 'Anyway, it's a Cretan legend, so a bull would have to come into it. Besides, Zeus was good at impersonating animals.'

'What a resourceful chap Zeus was,' said Hermione. 'Now a bull, now a shower of gold, fostered by a goat when he was a baby, turned into a ram to escape the monster Typhon — really, a human chameleon, you might say.'

'Wonderfully gifted at swallowing his children, too,' said Isobel. 'Wish he could teach *me* how it's done. A wonderful way to get rid of undesirable brats, and I could name a few, I can tell you!'

'There speaks the wolf in sheep's clothing which teachers have to be nowadays,' said Erica. 'More pie, anybody?'

It was just as the washing-up was finished that Ribble knocked on the cabin door.

'Oh, no!' said Isobel, opening the door in answer to Ribble's knock. 'Not you again, Inspector!'

'I'm afraid so, miss. May I ask whether you've got a visitor?'

'We're giving supper, bed and breakfast to a girl who was in this afternoon's folk-song and dance thing at Gledge End.'

'May I come in, miss? All I want is a word with Miss Pippa Marton.'

Pippa, who had caught her name, got up from the settee as Ribble walked into the lounge.

'Has one of them had an accident?' she asked anxiously.

'Why should you suppose that, miss?'

'Oh, don't be an ass!' said Isobel. 'One of them was killed only the other day. Can't you see she has been scared stiff that something else would happen? It was a perfectly reasonable question.'

'All I want to know,' said Ribble smoothly, ignoring Isobel's outburst and speaking to Pippa, 'is where the rest of your party were making for when they left the church hall.'

'We are booked in at the Youth Hostel at Lostrigg. Why? Do please tell me what has happened.'

'There's been an accident, I'm afraid, miss. I can't tell you more than that until I know a bit more myself. I think you would be better with your friends, miss, when I break the news to them. I can run you over to the Lostrigg hostel straight away.'

'I've got my bicycle here.'

'I will arrange for it, miss.'

'It's got a punctured tyre.'

'I daresay one of my men can cope with that.'

'Did they have an accident with the tandem?'

'No, miss.'

'Oh, for goodness' sake tell the poor girl what has happened!' cried Isobel. 'You can't leave it until you get her over to the hostel.'

'Very good, miss. First, Miss Marton, your brother has been injured, but he's going to be all right. We've got him to hospital and I've just been over there. He can't have visitors just at present, but you shall see him as soon as the doctors allow it. Don't worry on that score, miss. Lucky for him he was wearing a wig. It probably saved his life.'

'You mean he was attacked, like poor Judy?'

'That's the size of it. Miss Raincliffe, I'm very sorry to say, was not so lucky.'

Pippa, who had remained standing, collapsed on to the settee. Isobel sat down beside her and looked with hostile eyes at the detective-inspector.

'Dead, like the other one?' she asked, her arm round Pippa's shoulders. Ribble inclined his head.

'Only too much like the other one,' he said grimly, 'except that she must have met her attacker face to face. We shall have to hold all your company for a bit, Miss Marton, but I'll arrange everything.'

Pippa disengaged herself from Isobel. Her colour began to come back.

'Didn't they go off on the tandem, then?' she asked. Ribble shook his head. 'Were they — oh, so *that's* why we couldn't find them after the show! But why couldn't we? Where were they?'

'Still at the hall, miss.'

'So, if Peggy had not gone rushing off to find out what was keeping Micky —'

'One of your men might have stood a better chance than *she* did, yes, miss, but we can't be certain of that. If you would get your coat on, I think we ought to be going. I want to get to your friends before they go to bed. My car is just outside.'

'Can't you leave her here for the night?' asked the motherly Erica. 'We'll look after her.'

'No, I'd rather go. I *must* go,' said Pippa. 'Thanks all the same,' she added wanly.

'I'll tell you more about things on the way to Lostrigg,' said Ribble.

When Pippa had gone into the vestibule to put on her coat, Isobel said to him, 'Well, at least you can't suspect *us* any more.'

'Once the doctors were satisfied that what happened on the moor could not have been a hit-and-run accident, you were all in the clear, miss.'

'Thanks for nothing! You ought never to have suspected us in the first place!'

'We have to look at all sides of a question,' said Ribble mildly.

'It looks as though we could have saved my great-aunt a journey,' said Hermione.

'Your great-aunt, Miss Lestrange?' Ribble looked at her in sudden comprehension. 'Good gracious me! That couldn't be Dame Beatrice, could it?'

'Yes, of course it could,' said Isobel. 'She is coming here tomorrow to get us out of your clutches. At least, that was the idea, but it hardly seems necessary now.'

'I will let the Super. know and he will want to tell the Chief Constable. We all know Dame Beatrice by repute and it will be an honour to meet her,' said Ribble.

'All the same, it looks as though we could have saved her the journey,' repeated Hermione, 'since we are now in the clear without her help.'

'Ah, but I may be very glad of it myself,' said Ribble, 'if she will be prepared to assist me. I reckon I can do with a psychiatrist on the job. I'll call in at the station on my way to the hostel and mention that she is coming down. What time do you expect her, Miss Lestrange?'

'In the middle of the afternoon, I think. She will have lunch on the way and then come straight here before she goes to her hotel.'

'Then I'll come along, too, if I may.' He turned to Pippa, who had come back into the room. 'Well, miss, we'll be off. My car is outside.'

'Who on earth can be doing these awful things?' said Tamsin, when the inspector had taken Pippa away. 'Is it one of the dancers, do you think?'

'I don't know who else,' said Erica. 'I shall be glad when Monday is over. I've got to go to the inquest, as I was the one who actually saw that girl's body on the moor.'

# — 12 —

# YELLOW ARCHANGEL

'So what is all the brouhaha?' enquired Dame Beatrice, who had driven straight to the cabin on Sunday and had arrived at the time of siesta which followed the young women's Sunday lunch. *'Parlez lentement, doucement, en anglais* and, if possible, one at a time.'

'The floor is yours, Hermy One,' said Isobel. Hermione told the story of their troubles and told it well.

'But I think we've brought you here on a fool's errand, great-aunt,' she concluded. 'Something else has happened — we don't know all the details, but it's pretty bad and it's something the inspector knows we couldn't have done. We've discussed it, and it seems another one in that folk-dance party has been badly injured and another killed. One of them — one of the girls — ran off to find one of the boys after the show. The other girl was supposed to be staying the night here with us and some of what happened seems to have happened to her brother. He was the boy, she told us, who was thought to have gone off with the girl. She knew all about that before she left the hall. What she didn't understand, she said — she seems a simple, naive sort of bod — is why he went off in girl's clothes, but the inspector came and told her what really happened.'

'I mentioned transvestites,' said Isobel, 'but she sounded genuinely convinced when she said there was nothing of that sort about him. He had simply filled in for that girl who was killed so that the show could be presented more or less as they had rehearsed it. She told us that the other girl — Peggy she called her — had had her hooks in the brother for months and they thought she must have persuaded him to run off with her. It seems to have been a sort of Daisy Bell in reverse, because, although they were supposed to have taken the tandem on which brother Mick was usually the back-seat operator with another man in front, Pippa was sure her brother would not have been the instigator of the move, but, of course, it wasn't like that at all. Anyway, the inspector insisted — it amounted to that — on taking Pippa in his car to join her friends, so she didn't spend the night here after all, and that's all we know.'

'Oh, well,' said Dame Beatrice, 'you had better get your car and lead mine to the hotel I hope you have booked for me.'

'We booked you in at the Ewe and Lamb pub in the village. It's highly spoken of and has four bedrooms only, so we thought you would find it nice and quiet and it only takes about ten minutes in a car from here. Have you had any lunch? They only do snacks at lunch-time but we are told that Sunday dinner there is quite something. This is a holiday place, you see, and lots of the cabin people go there, so it flourishes.'

'I had lunch on the way up here, so perhaps you would all care to join me for dinner tonight, then.'

'*Would* we!' exclaimed Tamsin.

'She looks ethereal,' said her sister, 'but she's the prototype of the human boa-constrictor, and so I warn you.'

'Oh, come, now' said Hermione, 'be fair to the girl. The worst that can be said of her is that, like Bingo Little, she is apt to get a bit rough when in the society of a sandwich.'

'I'm not sure we ought to be joking,' said Erica very seriously. 'Two murders and very nearly a third don't make me feel exactly lighthearted and I've got to attend that inquest tomorrow and speak my piece about finding the body on the moor.'

'If the police are still conducting an investigation, the inquest will be adjourned as soon as the identity of the corpse has been formally established and the medical evidence given,' said Dame

Beatrice. 'Almost nothing will be required of you. If you so desire, I will accompany you. In any case I shall be interested to hear what the doctors have to say.'

Ribble came to the cabin at halfpast three and was introduced to Dame Beatrice.

'Our Superintendent has notified the Chief Constable of your arrival, ma'am,' he said, 'and they will be glad and honoured to meet you. May we take it that you will be willing, now you are on the spot, to put your great experience at our disposal?'

'What I have heard from these children,' replied Dame Beatrice, leering benevolently at the four young women, 'has aroused my interest, Inspector. I shall be delighted to put in my thumb.'

'Then, perhaps' — he, too, looked at the girls — 'I might have a word in private with you.'

'We can take any hint which is reinforced with the aid of a sledger-hammer,' said Isobel. 'Come along, children. We are being turned out into the snow.'

'If you ladies are going out, go in a car, keep together all the time, and on no account give anybody, male or female, a lift,' said Ribble impressively.

He waited until they were out of the cabin and even stood at the french doors to watch their departure towards the carpark, before he turned to Dame Beatrice and said, 'We can do with your help, ma'am. May I put my own version of the case before you? I expect the young ladies have told you something, but there are features in the case that they don't yet know about. There is a disordered mind at work. That's where we should welcome your co-operation. Somebody seems to have got it in for the young people who put on that song-and-dance show at Gledge End. The girl who was killed belonged to them and now one more of them has been murdered. Another is lucky to have escaped death, and this time there is no question of a hit-and-run car.'

'Then I can take it that you *really* have exonerated my great-niece and her friends?'

'Oh, yes, indeed. Apart from the fact that they could have had no hand in Saturday's nasty business —'

'Why not? They attended the performance.'

'They must have left the premises before the murderer did his job. A whole convoy of the cabin holidaymakers' cars left the carpark at the end of the show and I have evidence that theirs was among them and was sandwiched in, so to speak. I have witnesses who can swear to the number plates. Needless to say, my chaps have made a very careful check. There is only one direct road from Gledge End to the two-mile drive into the forest to get back to the cabins, and nobody deviated from it.'

'What about the car which brought up the rear of the procession? Couldn't that have slipped away without anyone being the wiser?'

'It was driven by an elderly lady who had a disabled passenger. I can't see how either of them, or both of them together, could have attacked two strong and healthy young people.'

'It seems unlikely, I admit.'

'There is another argument, anyway, regarding the first death, and one which a layman can't gainsay. The pathologist's report makes it clear that the girl was not knocked down by a hit-and-run car. Her injuries were only to the back of the head and were caused by repeated blows, probably from a heavy stone. We haven't found the stone but there are boulders on that part of the moor where the body was found, and we have found blood on the roadside near where her buckled bicycle was seen by the young ladies. We are going on the assumption that that was where she was killed. Then, as you may have heard, the murderer tried to conceal the body in a dip on the moor where two of the young ladies found it. The murders seem motiveless, so far as we can make out. If they are, it must follow that nobody is safe while this joker is at large. Of course the likely thing is that he is a member of the troupe. These last two attacks don't point anywhere else. My trouble is that one of my chief suspects was this second murdered girl. She, at least, seems to have had some sort of a motive, but, with her out of the way, there doesn't seem anything much to choose between the rest of them, although I have a leaning towards one of the men.'

'You stated that *two* more had been attacked. Who was the other one? My great-niece mentioned a brother of the girl who came here on Saturday evening.'

'A young fellow who did female impersonations for them, yes, the brother of this girl Pippa Marton. He was dressed as a girl, ready to have his photograph taken with the rest of the dancers, when he was set upon.'

'A fact which may be of the greatest importance, don't you think?'

'Oh, yes, I do. That's why we want your help. Our killer seems to have a Jack the Ripper personality, except that he doesn't mutilate the bodies. He leaves his trade-mark in the form of a poisonous toadstool pressed into the headwounds. Wouldn't you call that the act of a psycho, ma'am?'

'I shall know better when I have seen the dancers who are left. Meanwhile, since you are convinced of my own young people's innocence, I shall suggest to my great-niece and her friends that they return to their homes. You would have no objection to that, I take it?'

'Not so long as they leave me their home addresses, just in case. I may let the last girl in the concert party go home, too, for her own safety. The female impersonator who was attacked was her brother, as I said, and I have a theory that he may have been attacked in mistake for her. I hope not, because, if that is so, then I have to exonerate the rest of the group. The brother and sister are remarkably alike to look at, it is true, but none of their companions would have mistaken one for the other, so I'm inclined to think that the murderer made a mistake and that the sister was an intended victim, but that is only a hunch.'

'That is interesting. You prefer it to the other theory you outlined?'

'Yes, I do, ma'am, but there's a nigger in the woodpile in the person of the young fellow who used to ride tandem with the injured boy. Mind you, I'm not saying that their relationship was anything but what it ought to be, but there's a lot of that sort of thing about in these days, especially since the law was changed. The murdered girl — the first one — was sweet on the wounded boy and the second dead girl was, by all accounts, her rival. That part seemed straightforward enough, but to remove both of them would leave the way clear for this tandem partner, if you see what I mean, and that's a point I have to consider.'

'But why attack the beloved object as well as the predatory girls, Inspector?'

'Goodness knows, ma'am. Jealousy is as cruel as the grave, they say. That could be one answer, I suppose. He may have had his suspicions that his friend had paired off with one of the girls and left him flat.'

'I think I shall enjoy a chat with your dancers, Inspector.'

'You'll have a look at the young people, ma'am?'

'Oh, yes. It seems a pity to come all this way for nothing, does it not? I imagine you have questioned them closely about the first death?'

'Yes, I have. The only one of them who seemed to have an alibi was this girl Pippa. I know what is thought about alibis, ma'am, but this one seems unbreakable. I thought at first that I could eliminate two of the boys, but then I found I couldn't. They had spent most of the day in Gledge End getting the hall ready for Saturday's show, but I was unable to discover at what time they left, and the medical evidence hasn't been of much help, because the doctors can't say, within a couple of hours, when the first girl died. Now that we have eliminated your young ladies it has helped a bit, because there is no doubt the girl was dead when they found her. However, they weren't all that sure of the time they saw the damaged bicycle and when they had made their report and we had got the police surgeon along to look at the body, the best part of another hour had elapsed, which didn't help much. You see, my trouble is that I neither know when those two fellows left the church hall last Thursday nor at what rate they pedalled back. The death-spot wasn't all that far from Gledge End. At twelve mph they could have reached it in half an hour, I reckon, so I can't dismiss them from my calculations.'

'But your problem, I imagine, is not *only* that you cannot find out at what time they left the hall, or, presumably, whether they remained together when they had done so. What else?'

'There's another thing, yes. According to the rest of them, this Mrs Judy Tyne left the Youth Hostel, which is about twenty-five miles from where her body was found (if she followed the moorland road, as we think she did) at around nine in the morning. It could not have taken her six or seven hours to cycle that distance. This lot went everywhere on their bikes, so she must have been an experienced cyclist.'

'A puncture?'

'We don't think so. In fact, we're sure not. The tyres were quite tight. One of my chaps tested them. They were nearly new and there was no sign of a mend. The only damage was to the front wheel.'

'An assignation with somebody — with whoever killed her?'

'Must have been with one of the dancers, then, and it could have been with any one of them, including this second dead girl, but, of course, she's out of it now.'

'What was the alibi of the girl they call Pippa?'

'She was at Ramsgill's farm all day, sworn to by Mrs Ramsgill before she knew anything about the murder. I don't think it's any good trying to climb *that* tree, ma'am.'

'At what time did she leave the farm?'

'Round about tea-time, roughly speaking. Anyway, far too late for her to have got to where the body was found. Besides, she's a slip of a thing. Mind you, the doctors are going on the assumption that Mrs Tyne was struck from behind and probably taken by surprise, but, really ma'am, I can't see that Pippa Marton could have anything to do with it. Besides, there is this second death and also the vicious attack on her brother.'

'Come, now, Inspector! It is not unknown for sisters to attack their brothers.'

'I grant you he was attacked from behind, like the girl on the moor, but the second dead girl was face to face with the murderer and she would make two of Miss Pippa.'

'What about the other young men? Could they be connected with the first death, the death on the moor?'

'No real alibis at all. Two of 'em went to a swimming pool where nobody can swear to them, and the two on the tandem declare they went to the pictures, but again there is no real proof that they couldn't have slipped out, met the girl and killed her. But, there again, one of them is this boy who is now in hospital. Of course, the attack on him and the murder of the second girl need not have been by the same person that killed Mrs Tyne, or for the same reason. Against that, a death-cap toadstool was found pushed into all the three youngsters' headwounds.'

'Do you mean an extremely poisonous fungus which the botanists call *Amanita phalloides*?'

'I don't know what the botanists call it, ma'am, but I'm told it's pretty deadly. Anyway, it's convinced us that the murderer is a psycho and, if I may repeat myself, that is where we hope *you* will come in.'

'I am free as soon as I have registered at the Ewe and Lamb, where a room has been booked for me. I should like to begin work on the case at once. Can you pick me up there in half an hour's time? I am told it is quite near here.'

'I can drive you there, ma'am, and wait until you are ready to go.'

'Then I will leave a note here for my great-niece and we can be off at once. Is the death-cap toadstool readily obtainable in these parts?'

'Oh, yes, ma'am. I've had a word with the forest warden and he tells me that it grows under trees and that his foresters, who take the cabin holidaymakers around when they first come, are told to warn people about it and show them the difference between it and the mushroom which it somewhat resembles.'

'The death-cap, so named, seems reminiscent of the days when the judge in a case of murder was passing sentence, don't you think, and wore a black square on his august wig?'

'Yes, ma'am, that had occurred to me. Seems as though our fellow thought he was awarding the death penalty to those girls for some crime he thought they had committed. Wonder what was in his mind?'

'Murderers are as egoistic as the Roman emperors, Inspector. That is the answer here, I think, but speculation along those or any other lines is unprofitable at present.'

She scribbled in her small notebook, tore out the leaf and left it in the centre of the table for Hermione to find when the girls returned. At the Ewe and Lamb she registered at the desk and booked a table for five at dinner.

'Where first, ma'am, when we leave your hotel? For tonight I'm leaving the dancers at the Lostrigg Youth Hostel with a police-guard. The warden there wasn't any too pleased, as they were only booked in for last night, but he had to stretch a point for once and I promised to take them out of his care tomorrow. They will attend the inquest at Gledge End and then I shall escort them to the forest cabin I've been given.'

'Then I think I will wait to question them until after the inquest. Let us make first for the hostel at which they stayed previously. I should like a word with the warden.'

'That's at Long Cove Bay, ma'am, and only about half the distance to the Lostrigg place.'

'Good. I have to get back in time to dress for dinner and welcome my guests.'

On the way to the Youth Hostel Ribble detailed a conversation he had had with his Chief Constable when they had known that Dame Beatrice was to visit her great-niece. It had run: 'This is a very nasty business, Ribble.'

'Yes, indeed, sir. Not what I'm used to on our manor.'

'No, indeed. So what are you doing about those dancers?'

'I've commandeered an empty forest cabin for a couple of days to house them. I've no evidence against any of them except that all the boys' alibis for the first murder are suspect, but nothing points to one of them more than to the others. As for the girl, I want to get her right out of it, but I can't. On the evidence of Mrs Ramsgill, the farmer's wife, Miss Pippa Marton is in the clear so far as the death of Mrs Tyne is concerned, but there isn't an alibi in sight for this business at the church hall. None of them can produce one.'

'How's that, then?'

'Not one of them can swear to what any of the others were up to once the show was over. They were all lending a hand at clearing the platform and the body of the hall, removing their props, and so on and so forth, and some of the stuff was taken out of the hall and nobody can say who did what and who went where. Besides that, they're all scared stiff and are most unwilling to commit themselves to any definite statements in case they might incriminate themselves or one another. I was a bit doubtful about leaving Miss Marton with them, but I've got to keep them all rounded up until Dame Beatrice can take a look at them, and I thought my best plan would be to get them along to her as soon as I could.'

'Yes, I take your point about not leaving them on the loose. In any case, we couldn't expect Dame Beatrice to chase them all up when they got to their homes. You might be justified in holding them in custody for a couple of days, I suppose, but I think we shall get far more out of them if we don't frighten them further, or aggravate them too much. They are a pretty intelligent lot, I daresay, and probably know their rights and will exercise them, once they get over the shock.'

'I believe Dame Beatrice is expecting her secretary to join her. What about the other young women, sir, those who found the first body? We don't need them any more, do we?'

'If Dame Beatrice wants to send them home and it doesn't look as though they can help you any further, let them go.'

'I see the Newcastle chaps have picked up our man, sir.'

'Oh, yes, he's out of it all right. He'd still got the rucksack he stole from the Youth Hostel and he was wearing the anorak. Both have been identified and the lorry-driver who gave him a lift outside Durham has come forward. Our man couldn't have had anything to do with these last attacks and you never really considered him for the first one, did you?'

'Not after we were told about the toadstool. The thing is called the death-cap and seems to be this joker's trademark. We're up against a psycho all right, sir. That's why we can do with Dame Beatrice, as you say.'

'What about the young fellow who swears he saw the girl's car skid and hit a tree?'

'The girls don't know about that, sir, and I shan't tell them. Swore he saw the skid when he was on his way back from the forest carpark last Thursday and very cleverly identified the tree for us. Seems to be a bit of a woodman, not to say more than a bit of a naturalist. Name of Trent. Had one of the cabins and got to know the girls.'

So you didn't believe his story?'

'No, sir, but we'd given up suspecting the girls before he told it. I reckon he's sweet on one of them and told the lie about seeing the skid just to keep them out of trouble.'

'As my old schoolmaster, who was mad on Chaucer, would have said, "he was a verray parfit gentil knight".'

'And could have been a damned nuisance, sir, but no harm done on this occasion, as I had already made up my mind that those girls were out of it.'

'A bit of a naturalist, you say? Wonder what he knows about death-cap toadstools?'

'I'd never thought of that, sir. Well, the forest warden will have his address, so I can keep the tabs on him. Lies, even in what the liar thinks is a good cause —'

'Are not items to inspire confidence in the liar? I agree. Yes, keep your eye on him. Meanwhile, it will be interesting to see what Dame Beatrice makes of this business.'

'I shall give her some notes, sir, of visits I made in connection with the first murder and the outcome of same. I shall make my own enquiries with regard to the church hall affair and shall leave her to take her own course. We can compare our findings and discuss them later, if that is her wish. With her vast experience she may hit on something which I've missed. I hope she can. Unless one of those dancers is our man, or this young fellow who told me that unnecessary tarrididdle about Miss Lestrange's skid in the woods when she went to park the car, I haven't any line which looks like a useful follow-up.'

'Have you thought about that caretaker at the church hall?'

'In connection with the murder there, yes, sir, but I haven't questioned him yet from that angle. I've only taken his statement about finding the injured lad and the dead girl. I can see he might be implicated there, but it's difficult to see how he could have been involved in the death of that girl on the moor.'

'I would press him, all the same. Keep strictly within the rules, of course, and be sure to tell him that he is entitled to have his solicitor present — that should scare him a bit! — and see what he will come up with. After all, the part of the moor where the first body was found isn't all those many miles from Gledge End.'

# −13−

# ELDER

As they took the road to the hostel at Long Cove Bay, the car passed the spot where the first murder had taken place. Ribble pointed out the spot on the roadside verge where the damaged bicycle had lain.

'Interesting,' said Dame Beatrice. 'She was either cycling on the wrong side of the road or else she was returning to the rest of the party at Long Cove Bay, one would suppose.'

'Unless the murderer shifted the bike across the road, ma'am, but that seems unlikely. Our guess is that she had thought better of scarpering and perhaps had realised she had nowhere to sleep. They were booked in at Long Cove Bay for the Thursday and Friday nights, but not at the Lostrigg hostel until last night.'

'Do the Youth Hostels not take in benighted travellers?'

'It would be chancing your luck. They would, if they had room, I suppose, but, as I understand it, booking beforehand and in writing is the general rule. Besides that, she would have had another forty miles to cycle, even after she reached Gledge End, and she may well have baulked at that, especially if the wind was against her.'

Dame Beatrice had been conscious of the wind as soon as the car had come out upon the open moor. She looked out of the window at the rising slopes covered in dying heather and the sinister dark gold of acres of dead bracken and, through the windscreen, at the narrow serpentine road winding its way over the bleak autumn landscape. Further on there were patches of stone-walled pasture with here and there a shepherd's hut and a sheep-fold, sometimes whole, sometimes in ruins. But soon even this primitive evidence of human occupation was left behind, and when the car came in sight of the hostel, that, too, was sur-rounded by a waste of moorland. As a private house it had had a large garden for which many tons of soil had been imported from more fertile localities, but there was nobody at the hostel to give it the care, attention and hard work necessary for its preservation and unkeep.

Occasionally Mrs Beck made it one of the hostellers' chores to get to work on the gorse bushes, brambles, bilberries and crow-berries, and a bill-hook and secateurs were kept in the warden's cottage for this purpose. The job was an unpopular one, however, as the hostellers maintained, with some reason, that they were responsible for keeping the house tidy but that their obligations did not extend to the garden.

Ribble took Dame Beatrice straight to Mrs Beck's cottage. The warden was in and greeted Ribble with a grim smile.

'I expect you've heard we've had more trouble with your dance lot,' Ribble said.

'More trouble? I've heard nothing.'

'This is Dame Beatrice Lestrange Bradley. May we come in?'

'Happen you must. What's amiss now?'

Ribble told her.

'Dame Beatrice is consultant psychiatrist to the Home Office,' he said. 'We think we've got a homicidal maniac on our hands.'

'I should think so, too. Nobody's safe these days, are they?'

'I think you are wise to keep a dog,' said Dame Beatrice, giving the Alsatian her fingers to sniff. 'I wonder whether I might look at your register of guests? I am anxious to establish any possible overlaps.'

'Overlaps? Oh, I see what you mean. Folks that were staying with me at the same time as the dancers. It won't help you. The dancers came in last Wednesday evening and, except for poor Judy Tyne, stayed Thursday night and Friday night. I had nobody else except a party of four schoolteachers on Wednesday night and they went off first thing Thursday morning. I've had them before and I'm sure I can vouch for them.'

'Were they cyclists?'

'No, walkers. They couldn't possibly have picked up Judy on her bicycle.' Mrs Beck produced her records. Dame Beatrice took down the names and addresses of the teachers. They were all women and she could see why Ribble had not troubled, in his own phrase, to chase them up.

'The only help we might get from them,' she said, when she and the inspector were back in his car, 'is if they heard anything of the quarrel which caused Mrs Tyne to take herself off on Thursday morning.'

'I can find that out while you're busy on your own course of action, ma'am, but from what I've been able to find out, the row was nothing more than a cat-fight between Mrs Tyne and this other dead girl.'

'You spoke of what seems to be an alibi for the death of Mrs Tyne, Inspector.'

'Won't take five minutes, if you'd like to call on Mrs Ramsgill, ma'am.'

Mrs Ramsgill, like Mrs Beck, had not heard the news of the second death and the injury to Mick. She was deeply concerned.

'To think that Ramsgill and I were actually in that hall just before it happened!' she said. 'Well, I never did! How upset poor little Pippa Marton must be to think of her brother being set upon like that!'

'Ah, yes, Miss Marton,' said Dame Beatrice. 'She was with you on the day Mrs Tyne was killed, I believe.'

'Never went outside the door, once she got here, until she left at after five to go back to the hostel. Young Adam did his best to wheedle her into going out on the back of his motorbike, but she said she'd come to see *me*, not to go gallivanting.'

'Was the young man disappointed?'

'Oh, I don't really think so. He put on a bit of a show, but you know what boys are. If they can't get one girl, they know they can get another. That's what he did. Picked up a girl in a pub, he told me, and they had a champion time together.'

There was mist on the moors as Ribble drove Dame Beatrice back
to the Ewe and Lamb. She thought she had never gazed upon a
more desolate scene. The hills looked higher than they had done
on the outward journey, their outlines blurred and yet magnified
by the combination of eerie mist and the fading light.

She invited Ribble in for a drink when they reached the com-
fortable, friendly little hostelry, but he excused himself on the
grounds that he had paperwork to do when he got back to the
police-station.

'I'll pick you up and take you to where they are holding the
inquest,' he said. 'We shall ask for an adjournment, of course, so
the proceedings will be brief and we're not calling any of the
dancers this time. We shall need them later, I expect, when we
resume. After the inquest I shall have to go to the Lostrigg hostel
to pick up those young people and put them in their forest cabin.
Perhaps you would care to accompany me and get your first
impression of them.'

'You think one of them is your murderer, don't you?'

'Difficult to put anybody else in the picture. I shall have to see
the caretaker again, but I think I'll be wasting my time unless
something helpful has occurred to him now he's had time to think
things over. I wish, when I've got them treed in the forest (sorry
for the pun, I'm sure — not intended) you would have a real good
go at the five boys, ma'am. Not an alibi among the lot of them,
neither for the job on the moor or the murder at the hall. With a
mixed troupe like that, and most of them what you might call
artistic, there's no knowing what went on behind the scenes, is
there?'

Dame Beatrice agreed, but in an absent-minded way which
indicated that her mind was not entirely occupied with speculations upon the young men members of Wild Thyme.

The inquest next day was as formal as the inspector had
promised and in the afternoon he and she drove to the hostel at
Lostrigg. Its situation was very different from that of the house at
Long Cove Bay. It was surrounded by high green hills of a

benignity unimaginable after the bleak, forbidding uplands of the moors. The house itself was gracious, too, and was flanked by decidous woods, the trees showing brown, copper-coloured, gold and with some of their boughs still green. The mansion was double-fronted behind a beautifully-kept lawn, and the approach to the house was by an equally well-maintained broad gravel path. There were projecting wings to the house and beyond the trees were bright green upland pastures divided here and there by drystone walls.

The overall impression was one of peace, stability and moderate prosperity, and it was difficult to believe that the way to it had been by a road which writhed across the high moors and then made long sweeps and curves past isolated stone-built shepherd-huts until it reached the lower ground and entered the beginning of arable and pasture-land.

Ribble's driver pulled up at the side of the house and the other police cars, two of them, (for there were to be six passengers from the hostel), drew in behind him. Ribble and Dame Beatrice walked up to the front door of the hostel.

The warden this time was a man. Moreover, he lived on the premises, was married, and had a sitting-room, a bedroom and a private bathroom on the second floor of the building. He was a bearded, expansive individual and when he saw the police cars he went to the door himself.

'They're a bit restive, Inspector,' he said. 'I had to tell them you were coming again, otherwise I couldn't have kept them here. It's all a little bit off-beat, isn't it, wouldn't you say?'

'The warden, Dame Beatrice,' said Ribble. 'Mr Conyers, this is Dame Beatrice Lestrange Bradley. She is consultant psychiatrist to the Home Office and we are going to relieve you of the guests I mentioned over the phone.'

'I shall be glad to be rid of them. It's strictly against regulations to keep them here all day and all of yesterday, as I explained, but police business is police business, of course. You didn't give me any details when you brought Miss Marton along, but I gather the affair is serious.'

'About as serious as it can be,' replied Ribble. 'There may be a murder charge against one or more of them.'

'Good heavens! Come up to my sitting-room and I'll send for them.'

'Yes, they may as well hear what I've planned while they are all together. We can sort them out separately when we get them back to Wayland Forest.'

Given the news that they were virtually in custody, the remaining members of the Wild Thyme group were shocked into absolute silence for a minute or two. Dame Beatrice noted that they avoided one another's eyes. The first to speak was Willie, the dark Scot.

'But the tandem,' he said. 'It went, you know. What happened to the tandem? We thought the two of them had gone off on it until Pippa told us that Peggy was dead and Mick in hospital.'

'We shall find the tandem in good time, sir,' said Ribble. 'Well, now, we want you all to come back with us to Wayland Forest, as I said. I have accomodation for you there.'

'Oh, but, look here,' said Giles, 'our jobs, you know, and some of us are at College. We've got to clock in! Our half-term holiday ended yesterday.'

'You can notify the authorities, sir, and the Chief Constable will endorse your statements.'

'Oh, but, dammit, that's not good enough!'

'I ought to point out to you, sir, that I have the option of holding you in custody as suspected persons.'

'Suspected of what, for God's sake?'

'Murder is a very serious offence, sir.'

'Yes, but —'

'Let it go, Giles,' said Plum. 'No use kicking up a shine. Later on, when this ghastly business is cleared up, you can sue for unlawful arrest, but it's no good beefing now.'

'I am not arresting anybody as yet,' said Ribble, 'and for your own sakes, gentlemen, you will be well advised to co-operate with me. I have cars waiting outside.'

'What about young Pippa?' asked Peter.

'We shall take her with us, sir. Are you a particular friend of hers? If so, perhaps you would care to travel back with her and one of the other gentlemen. You, sir,' he said to Giles, 'will travel with Dame Beatrice and myself, and the rest will be accommodated in another police car.'

'What about our bikes?' demanded Plum.

˜ 'I will send a van to pick them up, sir, but you will not have access to them for a couple of days or so, for obvious reasons.'

'Oh, we shan't attempt to do a bunk,' said Ronnie. 'Personally I'm all in favour of a couple of days' extra holiday.'

The shock, Dame Beatrice saw, was wearing off. She was interested to note that there were no signs whatever of grief. Those must have worn off, too, if they had ever existed.

Over the Sunday night dinner at the Ewe and Lamb, Dame Beatrice had received a lively and more detailed account of the previous week's happenings than she had already gained. John Trent and, to a lesser extent, Adam Penshaw, came into the picture and so did further accounts of the Wild Thyme show.

Dame Beatrice added her quota of information and then said to Hermione, 'Laura will be here tomorrow. I shall be busy, I hope, as soon as she arrives and shall not be available to keep an eye on you. This murderer is one who appears to have a particular spite against young women —'

'One of the two dancers who was attacked on Saturday was a man, I thought you said.'

'He was dressed as a woman, dear child.'

'And made a remarkably good job of the impersonation, then. You could have fooled *me*,' said Isobel.

'He certainly seems to have deceived the murderer,' said Erica.

'Then why have the police rounded up the rest of them?' asked Tamsin. 'We've been talking things over since you went off with the inspector. They all knew this dead boy. *They* wouldn't have mistaken him for a woman. They knew he was putting on an act.'

'If he *looked* like a woman that might have been enough for the murderer. I mean, whoever has done these awful things must be completely insane,' said Hermione. 'Isn't that so?'

'Maybe, maybe not. There are legal definitions of insanity which may not coincide with your own. What I was about to do was to issue an order,' said Dame Beatrice, leering at her great-niece.

'I need only one guess. You gave me a pretty plain hint when you came to the cabin, didn't you? You want me to go home. But why should I? I don't know any of the Wild Thyme lot and none of them knows me. In any case you say the police have got the tabs on them. I'm not in any danger and there's nearly another week of our holiday to run.'

'Don't be silly, Hermy One,' said Isobel. 'If it were certain that one of the Wild Thyme lot had murdered two of the others you might have a point, but it isn't at all certain that one of them did. The police may have rounded them up as much for their own safety as because the inspector thinks one of them may be guilty. Another murder done elsewhere while they're incarcerated could put them in the clear. Anyway, if you want to know, Tamsin and I are going home tomorrow. *I* don't believe it was one of those dancers. Nobody breaks up a successful team by getting rid of two of its members and putting another one in hospital.'

'So speaks the schoolmistress,' said Erica, 'and I agree with her. The murderer is some sort of sex-maniac. That's clear enough. If you really want to know, our clinging burr, or even John Trent, is as likely a candidate as anybody else, and there may be a dozen other possibilities. There's plenty of motiveless violence about in these days, unfortunately.'

'I wish the police would put that girl under separate guard or let her go home,' said Tamsin. 'If it *is* one of the other Wild Thymers — and really I think it must be, so you can leave that stupid Penshaw and John Trent out of it — surely Pippa isn't safe while she's among them?'

'Well, of course, *she* could be the murderer,' said Hermione. 'She may have had it in for the other two girls and hated her brother, too. You never know with families. All right, Great-aunt, you win, but I'd much rather stay here and see the thing through.'

'You'd only be in the way,' said Isobel. 'Tell you what. Tamsin will go back to our parents and Erica will go home, so why don't you come back and spend the week at my flat with me? The murders have spoilt this holiday, anyway. We could have lots of fun together in London.'

'So there it is,' said Dame Beatrice to Laura, whom she had sent for to join her at the Ewe and Lamb. 'What do you make of it?'

'Three girls and six men make a rather lop-sided team, don't you think?'

'Especially, perhaps, when the girls provide the music and the men do most of the dancing.'

'Well, of course, morris and sword dances are male specialities. What else was on the programme?'

'According to Hermione, a dozen folk-songs in which all the members except the flautist took part, a solo sword dance by the Scottish lad —'

'Oh, yes, crossed claymores, I suppose.'

'— a sailors' hornpipe performed by two men and a girl, except that on this occasion the girl was a man in what the only remaining girl in the company referred to as 'drag' —'

'Oh, you've had speech with her, have you?'

'Yes, this morning at the forest cabin where the dancers have been lodged by the police while enquiries are being pursued.'

'What's the girl like?'

'I gathered that she is more apprehensive on her own account than grief-stricken because her brother has been injured.'

'That's interesting. Still, it does look as though it is the women in the party that the murderer is after.'

'Yes, indeed. The sister told me that when her brother was dressed as a girl it was difficult for anybody, even the members of the company, to tell them apart. I think there is little doubt that he was attacked in mistake for her.'

'In that case, won't the murderer have another go? It seems hardly safe to let her stay among the rest of them.'

'Unless, of course, Pippa Marton herself is the killer.'

'And had it in for the other two girls? But what about her brother? Could he have found out that she was a murderess and so she had to try to eliminate him for her own sake in case he shopped her to the police?'

'Any number of wild surmises can be made. The trouble with this one is that, unless the farmer's wife is lying, the girl cannot have killed the first young woman. For that death she has a complete alibi.'

'Alibis, like promises and eggs, are made to be broken.'

'This one seems to be particularly sound.'

'In other words,' said Laura, 'you don't believe she did it. Well, I must say that knocking holes in people's heads doesn't seem the method a girl would choose for disposing of those she doesn't like, so Pippa passes, I suppose.'

'Are we overlooking Jael, the wife of Heber the Kenite? When I have questioned the girl further, I may go to see the farmer's wife again.'

'And try to bend her round to your way of thinking?'

'In these latitudes, as you should be well aware, such effort would be wasted. People up here are not malleable.'

'They cling to their opinions with the single-minded tenacity of limpets clinging to rocks, you mean. Yes, I suppose they do. What's my part in all this?'

'The humble but essential office of scribe. I do not care to use a tape-recorder. People distrust them'

'Well, they are a kind of bugging device, I suppose.'

'And, being evil-minded, as all mechanical contraptions, in fact, all inanimate objects, are, they may go wrong at crucial moments. I prefer the written word, even though it does not appear originally in longhand.'

'Forward, Sir Isaac Pitman,' said Laura. 'You say you're sending those four girls home. Didn't Hermione chafe a bit? She's an independent young madam, I thought, as a general rule.'

'Fortunately Hermione is in no position to object to her deportation. The cabin is booked in the name of Miss Erica Lyndhurst and she agreed with me that the four of them are better out of the way.'

'But why? You must have said something which convinced her.'

'Oh, I did.'

'Any use asking what it was?'

'I took her aside and told her that the greatest danger was to the young Tamsin Lindsay. I thanked her for upholding my authority and advised her to vacate the forest cabin forthwith. They left this morning.'

'I don't get it. Could you supply chapter and verse, or is it one of those guessing games?'

'By no means. When we have heard the stories which the dancers have to tell and can co-relate them with what I have heard already from the cabin party, you will know as much as I do and, I have little doubt, will come to the same conclusion as I have done.'

'You know my methods, Watson. Apply them,' said Laura.

'Right. Fair enough. When do we start?'

# -14-

# TWAYBLADE

Pippa reminded Dame Beatrice of Tamsin, for the girls had three things in common. They were much of an age, both were in a state of alarm and uncertainty and both were artists, Pippa with her flute, Tamsin with pencil and brush.

The young men had been asked to remove themselves to the bedrooms while Dame Beatrice interviewed Pippa in the sitting-room of Ribble's requisitioned forest cabin in which a police-woman had been Pippa's companion.

'None of us did it, you know,' said Pippa defensively. 'I mean, how could we? We were all together all the time.'

'You are referring to Saturday afternoon. What can you tell me about the previous Thursday?' Dame Beatrice asked.

'Oh, well, we weren't together then, of course. We didn't rehearse until after tea. We wouldn't have rehearsed then if things had been normal. It was Judy going off and not coming back which upset things.'

'You yourself spent the day on a farm, I believe.'

'Well, only in the farmhouse, actually. Mrs Ramsgill will tell you.'

'Was the farmer at home?'

'No, only to lunch. She said he wouldn't be coming back much before six, so I didn't wait to see him again. Oh, but he had nothing to do with Judy's death. He had never even met her, so far as I know.'

'You did not, any of you, go to the farm for butter or eggs or milk?'

'Oh, that? I didn't think that counted and anyway it wouldn't have been Mr Ramsgill we saw. It would have been Mrs Ramsgill or the dairymaid.'

'Ah, yes, of course.'

'Detective-Inspector Ribble told us that you would be coming. He said you are a psychiatrist. Does he think one of us is mad?'

'My work is concerned more with the emotionally disturbed than with what you would call the insane,' Dame Beatrice replied. She nodded to Laura, who was poised, a shorthand notebook in front of her. 'Now, Miss Marton, we come to last Saturday. Will you give me an account of your whole day until the time you reached Miss Lyndhurst's forest cabin? There is no need to elaborate. Just give me the plain facts, please, and answer my questions as accurately as you can.'

'Are you going to question our men as well as me, to make sure we all tell the same story? You see, I shall have to include what others did, and they would have to tell about me,' said Pippa.

'Just tell the story in your own way. I am trained to separate the wheat from the chaff.'

'When will they let me see my brother?'

'I cannot say. Meanwhile, please render me all the help you can. The sooner the police apprehend his aggressor, the safer this part of the world will be for everybody.'

'Poor Peggy!'

'Yes, indeed. Her sudden appearance in that dressing-room may have saved your brother's life. I also think she may have seen her murderer face to face.'

'So you want to know who else might have gone into that room besides Peggy after the show was over. My account won't help you. I'm sure that, whoever killed Judy and Peggy, it wasn't one of our lot.'

'It's a dirty bird that fouls its own nest. Your loyalty does you credit, but is not likely to be helpful.'

'It isn't loyalty. It's absolute conviction.'

'So be it. At what time did your Saturday begin? We may exclude breakfast.'

'We didn't get away from Mrs Beck and the hostel much before ten. Ten o'clock in the morning is the deadline, you see, for hostellers. The boys had loaded up the trailer which carried costumes and props — the wooden swords, Willie's claymores and kilt, the morris sticks and all the rest of the gear. We had put all those things ready the night before, so that the trailer had only to be hitched on behind the tandem in the morning. All our individual private gear had to be left till last. The men's bikes have those long, capacious leather holdalls, but we, the girls, have only a smallish saddlebag behind us and a basket on the handlebars, but everybody carries a rucksack or a haversack as well.'

'So you left at about ten.'

'And rode our bicycles straight to Gledge End and took over the church hall as arranged. We needed a rehearsal because, except for Giles and Plum, who had gone over on Thursday to arrange the seating, none of us had seen inside the place to know how much space was available for the dances or where the piano and the musicians were going to be put. We had a picnic lunch in the hall, then a rest for about an hour after we'd swept up the crumbs —'

'You swept the floor?'

'Oh, yes. Giles found a soft broom in the broom cupboard where — well, you know.'

'Yes, I know. So Giles knew that the cupboard was unlocked. Did any of the rest of you know?'

'He came back into the hall with the broom and Plum took it back and put it away, so he would have known.'

'Oh, well, I shall be talking to both of them later on.'

'Then we rehearsed and had another rest and then we changed for the songs and I put on my beard and the caretaker came to ask whether we were ready to open the doors for the audience to come in, and that's about all I know.'

'I see. My next question is important, so please answer it carefully. You may prove to be extremely helpful. Your part in the programme was as flautist, you told me, with an occasional gravitation to the piano. Did you at any time notice whether anybody in the audience left the hall during the performance?'

'I wouldn't know whether anybody left during the last item because I was doing the hobby-horse and I had to concentrate like mad so that I didn't get in the way of the dancers. I hadn't a chance to notice anything except what they and I were up to.'

'Yes? Well, now, to return to my vital question: you may not have noticed anybody leaving the hall during the last item, but what about earlier on?'

'I think one or two slipped out, but I never notice the audience when I'm playing. You don't, with a flute, you know. It's sheer concentration on my part.'

'Did you recognise anybody in the audience when they first came in?'

'Oh, yes. Farmer and Mrs Ramsgill came. They brought their lodger with them, but they didn't all sit together. Perhaps they had not bought the same priced seats. Adam — the boy who has been lodging with them — went up on to the platform first of all, but was soon headed off, so I suppose he took umbrage, as he did when I wouldn't go out with him. When I looked up from arranging my music I noticed that he had taken an absolutely back seat near the door. I think he is rather a spoilt, sulky boy. He didn't take it too well at all when I wouldn't sit on the pillion of his motorbike.'

'When was this?'

'Last Thursday when I was visiting the farm.'

'Ah, yes, everything seems to go back to that Thursday.'

'You mean because that was when Judy . . .'

'Yes, indeed. Well, Miss Marton, I think that is all. I will arrange for you to see your brother as soon as the doctors allow him to have visitors.'

'We weren't all that close, but . . .'

'Of course you are anxious about him. Oh, there is one other thing. Would you prefer to be lodged separately, away from your companions?'

'Oh, please, no! I know the police think one of us killed Judy and Peggy, but we didn't. I'm positively *certain* we didn't.

There's a criminal lunatic at large and the police have got to find him before other people get killed.'

'I sympathise with your point of view, but is it not significant that nobody outside your company seems to have been attacked?'

'I know it looks bad for us, but have the police found the tandem?'

'An apt answer to my question and one which goes some way towards proving your point. Could any of your party have been absent long enough from the rest of you to have pedalled it away? Please set aside your prejudices and answer me accurately.'

'We are all pretty good cyclists and a man, especially, could get quite a long way, even riding the tandem solo, in under five minutes, but then he would have had to walk back to the hall, and I'm sure nobody was absent for as long as that.'

'Has your group, so far as you know, made any enemies?'

'Enemies? No. Some gang once tried to rough us up, but Plum is a heavyweight boxer and Willie is a black belt, so nothing came of it, and we never give our shows at night, anyway, and that's when trouble starts.'

'Would either Mrs Tyne or Miss Raincliffe have had, perhaps, a jealous lover?'

'Not so far as I know. Judy was married, of course, but separated. I can't really imagine anybody fancying Peggy, but, of course, you never know. I think my brother was her last hope, but she didn't make first base, as the Americans say, with him. The only company Micky wants at present is Willie's. He admires him very much. They are not gay. It's hero-worship and when Mick is older he'll get over it and settle down with a girl, I'm sure. Willie has got a girl, anyway, but he likes Mick and acts as a father to him, and to anybody as weak as Mick it's real protection. We're orphans, you see, and Willie manages Mick's finances for him. Willie teaches economics at a polytechnic and is ever so good with money matters.'

'The Scottish blood, perhaps?'

'Oh, Willie is a Highlander, but I believe his mother comes from Peebles. He is a very quiet boy, but the rest of us respect him.'

'You must forgive my next question, and I shall understand if you refuse to answer it. Is it possible that your brother, in a fit of irritation, could have attacked Miss Raincliffe and then hit himself on the back of the head to make it look as though he himself had been attacked?'

Instead of the indignant denial which might have been assumed, Pippa considered the question.

'He might have attacked Peggy,' she said, after a pause. 'She made herself an awful nuisance to him. I don't believe he would have hit himself over the head as a cover-up, though, anyway, not so hard as to make himself a hospital case. He is a physical coward and, besides that, Peggy was much heavier and stronger than he. You think Peggy and the murderer met face to face, but Micky would never have risked having a go at her if that was so. He wouldn't have stood a chance. Oh, no, to fight anybody wasn't and never will be Micky's scene.'

'So what do we make of Miss Pippa Marton?' asked Dame Beatrice, when Pippa had been released.

'That she doesn't think much of baby brother and isn't all that fond of him,' Laura replied. 'As for the rest of what she said, I don't think she knows who killed the two girls, but she certainly seems to dismiss any suggestion that it could be one of her own lot.'

'And your own opinion about that?'

'I can't express one until we've seen the rest of them.'

'Cautious woman! Would you step to the door which Miss Marton has just closed behind her and ask for Mr Giles Tranmire?'

Giles, conscious of his position as the leader of Wild Thyme, was in a state of mild indignation.

'Look here, you know,' he said, 'by what right are we held here like this? What about the liberty of the subject and all that, you know?'

'Yes, I do know, and I sympathise,' said Dame Beatrice. 'The alternative, however, has been pointed out to you. The police are permitted to hold you in custody for forty-eight hours as suspected persons. You would not prefer it to be in a police-cell, would you? Sit down, Mr Tranmire and let us get on with the business. "The sooner it's over, the sooner to sleep," as the Reverend Charles Kingsley somewhat optimistically stated. Are you capable of unbiased thinking?'

'No. If you're going to ask me which of our lot could have killed those two girls and bashed up young Mick, my answer is that any of us *could* — I mean, we were all *there*, so to speak — but none of us *did*.'

'You and Mr Redman are one another's alibi for the first murder, I believe?'

'Old Plum may look like an all-in wrestler, but he wouldn't hurt a fly.'

'I wonder why a fly is chosen for that particular tribute to a person's gentle nature? No matter. Thank you, Mr Tranmire.'

'Is that all, then?'

'Oh, yes. Would you send in Mr Nicolson?'

'I have given the matter some thought, as is the way of it with me,' said Willie, when he had seated himself, 'and my thought is that the tandem is at the root of the mystery.'

'That is interesting, Mr Nicolson. Would you care to enlarge upon that statement?'

'I'll do that. The theft of the tandem was no wanton matter of person or persons concerned with stealing a means of transport. It was calculated to deceive the police into thinking that two persons were involved in the crime.'

'And from this you deduce?'

'Ask yourself, woman! At the time when Peggy was killed and wee Micky injured — and if ever I get my hands on whoever did *that* —!'

'Yes, at the time when . . .?' Dame Beatrice prompted him.

'Well, now, there were the two of them, away from the rest of the party, leaving six of us in the main hall. The photographer was getting impatient and soon left us, we five men and the lassie. Do you not think it would have been very noticeable if another of us had absented and gone into the changing-room just then?'

'You are going on the assumption that the attacks on Miss

Raincliffe and Mr Marton took place at approximately the same time, are you?'

'They could only have been minutes apart and I will be prepared to swear, in court or anywhere else, that the six of us were together in the hall while those attacks were taking place.'

'How long was Miss Raincliffe absent before you all decided that she and Mr Marton had taken the tandem and gone off together?'

Willie shook his head. A matter of minutes, he thought. He added that he, for one, could not bring himself to accept what, at the time and before Peggy's body was found, the others had thought, that the two had gone off together.

'He could not thole the lassie any one way,' he said, 'but there it was. No sign of either of them and, when we went to get our cycles, the tandem gone. What were the others to think? And the back door to the changing-room wide open at that.'

'Miss Raincliffe's body was hidden in the cupboard, of course, a cupboard to which, I understand, Mr Tranmire and Mr Redman had had separate access before the performance began.' She waited for a response to this statement, but Willie remained impassive, so she went on: 'As the back door was wide open, was it not strange that the caretaker seems to have found Mr Marton unconscious in the bushes, whereas none of the rest of you noticed him there?'

'When we found the dressing-room empty and the door open which had been shut and bolted before the show began, the others jumped to conclusions. Then, when we found the tandem gone, too, and the time getting on and ourselves due at Lostrigg by ten o'clock and forty miles to go, well, I could understand what the rest of them thought, loth though I was to believe it, as I will be telling you.'

'But surely you must have believed what appeared to be the evidence of your own eyes?'

'The lassie was strong-willed and resolute. I was all the while trying to put out of my mind a suspicion that she had killed Judy, but the others thought maybe she had asserted herself over Mick and carried him away.'

'The captive of her bow and spear?'

'The tongue that lassie had on her you would scarce believe. She could wheedle, aye, and she could scold. The others doubted whether she had been too much for the poor laddie. As for the caretaker, we have been told very little, but I would take it as a mathematical certainty that from the first he had his suspicions of that open back door and went out to see what it was all about, and had a better look round than Giles had done.'

'Yes, the back door is interesting. Who opened it, do you suppose? It must have been one of your own party. Nobody else had access to it from the inside.'

'That will have been Mick. He is claustrophobic. He rallied when the rest of us were there, but, left by himself, my theory would be that he not only opened the door, but stepped outside to get some air and found the murderer lurking.'

'But why? Why should he have been lurking?'

'Is it that you think I can read his mind? Maybe he was hoping the door would be opened and he to get inside and steal any money we had.'

'Well, that didn't seem to yield much,' said Laura, when the rest of the members of Wild Thyme had been interviewed. 'What comes next?'

'My recommendation to Inspector Ribble to check on the home addresses these young people will have given him and then to release them. If anything more transpires he can always apply to them again. It was purely for our convenience that they were gathered together here. There is really no good reason for detaining them any longer.'

'If I had to pick one of them out for further questioning, it would be my compatriot Nicolson, sorry though I am to say so. I always think there's something not too healthy about this 'wee laddie' protective stuff. It's all right when it's women. Most of us, I guess, have a strong mother-complex, but between men it's more than a bit fishy, don't you think?'

'Miss Marton stated, without being asked, that Nicolson and Marton were not 'gay', but I think your point is a valid one. We have to face the fact that both the women who wanted to mother Mr Marton have been murdered, and, after all, murder is a final solution when it comes to getting unwanted persons out of the way.'

'All the same,' said Laura, 'you don't think Nicolson did it, do you?'

'I have Inspector Ribble's notes to go on. First, it seems that it could have been only by the most extraordinary coincidence either that the two men met Mrs Tyne on the moors that Thursday and killed her, or that one or other of them did.'

'Yes, you let me see the notes, but there doesn't seem any proof of how Nicolson and Marton actually spent that Thursday. Some bits of their story Ribble seems to have been able to check, but there still seems to be a lot of time unaccounted for, except for their own uncorroborated explanations.'

'True, but I would be far more suspicious of a story which dove-tailed in every particular. As for the affair at the Gledge End church hall, we are given no evidence whatever that Nicolson could have killed that woman, still less that he would have injured his protégé.'

'Do you think claustrophobia accounted for that door being opened?'

'It is possible. Far more likely, though, that the murderer knocked and Mr Marton let him in.'

'So where *do* we go from here?'

'To place Miss Pippa Marton under police protection as soon as Inspector Ribble, under directions, no doubt, from his Chief Constable, tells these young people that they are free to go. Then I want to talk to Miss Tamsin Lindsay, John Trent and my great-niece. I have a feeling that they are the people who can convince me that I have come to the correct conclusion.'

'Do you mean that you can name the murderer?'

'I can produce a name, yes. Proof is a different matter. The evidence I have gathered is purely psychological and would never be accepted in a court of law. This is a classic case of rejection followed by vengeance.'

'So it's a woman's crime?' asked Laura. 'I could believe that if I didn't know that both the obvious murderers are dead.'

# −15−

# TROMPETTE DES MORTS

'I don't see why Erica should know something the rest of us weren't told,' said Hermione, when she and Isobel were in the latter's London flat, 'or why my great-aunt made us promise not to ask her any questions.'

'Erica wouldn't have answered them, anyway,' said Isobel. 'She has been trained to keep her head closed when delicate negotiations are to be undertaken. I can tell you one thing, if you really want to know. I'm pretty sure Dame Beatrice told her the name of the chief suspect.'

'But why should she have done that?'

'Obviously to make sure that Erica gave up the tenancy of the cabin and so got the four of us out of the forest toot sweet.'

'But why?'

'Because we are of feminine gender and the murderer seems to have a down on defenceless females.'

'Yes, but only on the defenceless females in the Wild Thyme gang. There is no suggestion that he has ever attempted to attack anybody else.'

'There is time for that, I suppose.'

'It *must* be one of that lot. I wonder which? What bothers me is that boy who has been taken to hospital. I know he was dressed as a girl when he was set upon, but none of his own set would have mistaken him for one.'

'I think the likely explanation is that, when the real girl was set upon by the murderer, he went to the rescue, got clobbered and then the murderer returned to the task in hand and finished the girl off.'

'So this boy would know the murderer. If so, he'll be in a very dangerous position once he is in circulation again.'

'Oh, the police will have got the name from him and made their arrest long before he is discharged from hospital,' said Isobel confidently.

'But he must have been attacked from behind, it's thought. Do you like pigs?' asked Hermione.

'The *non sequitur* of the century! I've never asked myself. I like bacon and ham and the occasional cut from a good joint of pork — don't get much chance of that. Living alone, I rely on chops and steaks. But pigs? I don't believe I have ever been acquainted with any.'

'I wondered whether you'd care to come to Stanton St John for a day or two, to finish the holiday. I should like to invite the other two as well. It seems a pity to break up the party before the end of the week. What do you think? Erica gave me her phone number before we split up, and you've got it, too, I suppose. Should we ring her? Just as you like, of course.'

'I *do* like pigs,' said Isobel. 'I dote on them. Oh, yes, do ring her, Hermy! It's a great idea. The only thing is — well, for all four of us to descend on your parents seems a bit much, doesn't it?'

'Heavens, no! My mother adores having the house full of people, and we've plenty of room to put up a dozen guests. My father is never happier than when he is showing off the pig population to anybody who will go the rounds with him, and so I know he will be glad to see us. Isobel —' She broke off and gazed at her friend, her eyes alight and wide open.

'Say on. You have our ear,' said the older woman.

'Isobel, why did my great-aunt insist that Tamsin should not go to her own home until the murderer is caught?'

'Oh, you know Tamsin. She has given John Trent her home address.'

'John Trent? Oh, but, surely —'

'I know. I can't believe it, either.'

'It *couldn't* be John!'

Isobel shrugged her shoulders and looked out of the window at the grey London sky.

'Why should John have told those lies about seeing you skid the car into that tree?' she said. 'If it had been Tamsin I could understand it. She's crazy about him, you know, and, being about as goofy as they come, she makes no secret of the fact, but why should he tell lies to the police to keep *you* out of trouble?'

'Not, as you so tactfully point out, because of my womanly charm, but because of his own chivalrous nature, I suppose. Let's phone mother and then Erica, shall we?'

'The Ewe and Lamb first, dearie. I am so much impressed by Dame Beatrice that I don't take any further steps without her knowledge and consent. She told us about John's lie.'

Laura took the call and relayed it to Dame Beatrice, for they had just finished dinner when the message came through.

'An excellent plan,' said Dame Beatrice, when she had gone to the telephone. 'I hope you will all have an enjoyable few days at Stanton St John. Tell nobody where you are going and ask Miss Tamsin Lindsay and Miss Erica Lyndhurst to leave no forwarding address. These are probably unnecessary precautions, but, as I have heard it said, better to be safe than sorry.'

'There is something I'm dying to ask you, great-aunt, but I don't suppose you would answer me.'

'No, I would not, at this juncture. Let us say, in Laura's elliptical phrase, that your guess is as good as mine.'

'I don't believe that's true.'

'How right you probably are. Goodbye, my child, and bless you.'

The girls had split up into couples immediately the inquest on Judy Tyne was adjourned and they were free to leave the forest region. The telephone conversation was held on the same evening, Monday, and by tea-time on Tuesday, the day on which Dame Beatrice had concluded her interviewing of the members of Wild Thyme, the four from the forest cabin were reunited at Carey Lestrange's farmhouse at Stanton St John in Oxfordshire.

Following this, events at the Long Cove Bay hostel and in Wayland forest took a new turn. The first intimation of this came to Ribble's notice by way of a telephone call from the police station at Long Cove Bay itself. It was to the effect that the police there had been told of a broken window in the Youth Hostel and the theft of the warden's records.

'Wouldn't bother you with this except that you've had trouble over that group of folk-dance people with two of them murdered, and they all stayed at the hostel and were resident there when the first girl was killed,' the message ran. 'Don't suppose there's any connection, but thought we would let you know.'

Ribble who, with his sergeant, had been making so-far fruitless house-to-house enquiries at Gledge End in an attempt to trace the missing tandem, gave up the quest temporarily and went over to the hostel.

Mrs Beck was in her cottage.

'I reported it because of the broken window and my register gone,' she said. 'Nothing else missing? Well, there wouldn't be, would there? I never leave any money there and, as it happens, I didn't have any hostellers that night. Time of year, you see. Folks don't much fancy walking or cycling on the moors when it comes near to November. Besides, these murders have been in all the papers. The nuisance I've had to put up with from reporters! You the same, I suppose, Inspector. But who on earth would want to make off with my registers?'

'I suppose somebody wanted some names and addresses, Mrs Beck.'

'To burgle their houses? Seems far-fetched to me. You don't find well-off folks using the hostel. They would stay at hotels, wouldn't they? My members' homes wouldn't be worth burgling.'

'You never know, Mrs Beck.'

His private opinion, expressed later to Dame Beatrice was: 'If your ideas are the same as mine about this business, ma'am, I reckon this latest effort is an attempt to throw dust in our eyes. He had no need to steal the hostel register because, to my way of thinking, he already had stayed there. He would have had ample opportunity, if so, to take a look at the books, and most likely no need to do so, anyway, since he already knew the address he wanted. This must have been to try to make out that he had never seen the register or been in the hostel before. The Long Cove Bay chaps have had a look for the record, but ten to one it's in the sea by now, and no use to anybody.'

'Have you any news about the missing tandem?'

'Nothing helpful, no, ma'am. Several people saw a man riding it solo, but nobody seems to have taken enough notice of it to be able to describe him and the different opinions as to which direction he was taking are enough to drive me haywire. He certainly didn't ditch the tandem anywhere near Gledge End, or we would have found it by now.'

'It looks less and less like one of the Wild Thyme dancers, don't you think?'

'So you've hinted before, ma'am, and I don't want you to name me any names. I can't pre-judge the case and I've got to get sufficient evidence to produce in court. I take it that you can't supply me with that?'

'Most unfortunately, no, I cannot, and you are right not to allow prejudice to distort your mind.'

'That Willie Nicolson distorts it, ma'am. He's a Highlander and that race are apt to be very dark horses compared with the likes of you and me. Devious is the word.'

'My secretary is a Highlander, and a more open, and, in every way, a more ingenuous woman, I have yet to meet.'

'The ladies come outside the scope of my argument, ma'am. I'm only saying that Nicolson was the owner of that tandem.' He chuckled and rang off, but there was soon another story to be told and it concerned another set of records, this time those of the forest warden. When she heard of this, Dame Beatrice confessed to Ribble that she was perturbed.

'There is only one interpretation to be put upon these two thefts, Inspector,' she said. 'Our murderer is what my secretary would call 'in business' again.'

'You may well be right, ma'am, and a very nasty business it is. What's in his mind, do you suppose?'

'Revenge,'

'Sounds more like a foreigner, then.'

'Well, the English are not good at hating, but, unlike Bottom, who could merely gleek, no doubt they can murder, upon occasion.'

'And the Scots, ma'am?'

'Ah,' said Dame Beatrice, 'I see that you are still barking up the same tree. 'Out with your man and set him against the wall.' Your mind still runs on Mr Nicolson.'

'It would, if I had a little more to go on,' said Ribble. 'He has no alibi for the first murder and, as I see it, the rest of them would lie themsleves black in the face to cover up for him for the second one.'

The story told by the forest warden was similar, in many respects, to that told by Mrs Beck. Having received his telephone call, Ribble went to see him.

'You know the set-up here, Inspector,' he said. 'Non-residents are entitled to enter the forest on payment of a toll, so although we have a check on all the cabin parties, we have virtually none on our occasional visitors. However, I really can't think that one of these could be responsible for the disappearance of my records. I mean, somebody just passing through could have no possible interest in them.'

'What records would these be, sir? Names and addresses of your cabin people?'

'Exactly. I need them for reference and, in any case, they are nobody else's business and are not in any way what one may call confidential. Why should anybody take my records?'

'You don't suspect any, in particular, of your tenants, I suppose, sir?'

'Nobody in particular, but it is possible, I suppose, that one of the younger men might want to check the address of a young woman who had taken his fancy.'

'Was any damage done, sir?'

'The window-catch on the ground floor — my office is on the ground floor with my flat above it — the window-catch had been forced, so I suppose the intruder climbed in by the window. The door has a Yale lock and there had been no tampering with that. No, there was no actual damage. I have no lock on my desk or to any of the drawers in it, and I have never troubled to lock my filing-cabinet as it never contains anything of a strictly confidential nature or anything of value. Money is never left on the premises. I need hardly tell you that.'

'When did you miss the records, sir?'

'Immediately before I telephoned you. I have my routine and I adhere to it. My office hours — that is to say, the times when I am available for interviews or to listen to complaints — are from nine until eleven each morning and from five o'clock to six each afternoon. I very seldom get complaints, but I like to welcome new residents on the first evening of their stay. As for my morning sessions, they are devoted to paperwork and sometimes to checking on those visitors who propose to take the long forest trail. As you probably know, there are four marked trails in the forest. One is a short walk which takes about three-quarters of an hour, the second and third take from an hour and a half to two hours. There are coloured route-signs which are simple to interpret. The long trail, however, covers ten miles and we like to know at what time the walkers set out and we ask them to clock in at the office when they get back.'

'So you check in this way in case anybody gets lost, I suppose.'

'That is the idea. They can hardly get lost unless they stray from the marked course, but part of it is in open country and then, if the mist comes down suddenly, or if they loiter too long and it gets dark, well, then they can be in trouble and we advise them before they start to stay put until the search party finds them if they do get lost or benighted.'

'Yes, sir, very interesting, but what about the theft of your records? You telephoned me at ten this morning and you say you did so as soon as you discovered the records were missing. Could I have the whole story?'

'Oh, certainly, but there is not much I can add to what I said over the phone. We let the cabins on a weekly basis from Saturday to Saturday. We don't encourage people to clock in before lunch because the cabins are cleaned when the outgoing tenants leave at

ten or earlier on the last Saturday of their stay. Some people book
for a week, others for longer. A fortnight is the average in the
summer, a week in Spring or at this time of year.'

'So in mid-week you would not be as busy as at weekends,
whatever time of year it was.'

'That is correct. I left the office at six last evening when everything was still in order and came in at nine this morning as usual. I
did not take my records out of the filing-cabinet immediately, as I
had some odds and ends of correspondence to clear up and that
involved nothing but opening my desk.'

'May I look at your filing-cabinet, sir? Detective-Constable
March will check it for fingerprints. We have some from a break-
in at the Youth Hostel at Long Cove Bay which we should like to
match.'

'You mean the same man broke in there?'

'We shall know when we have the prints.'

'But a person who would use a youth hostel is hardly a person
who would book accomodation in the forest, Inspector. Aren't
the hostellers birds of passage? Here, you know, we never take
bookings of less than a week, except —'

'Except when the police commandeer a cabin for a couple of
days. Yes, I know. Much obliged for your help in that little
matter, sir.'

'Oh, I made the books tally up to a point. I recorded your
dancers as having been accomodated in the cabin evacuated at the
beginning of the week by those four women who went off at such
short notice. The cabin had been paid for, you see, and they were
not entitled to any reimbursement, neither did they ask for any.
Your dance people did not occupy that particular cabin, but it
tidied things up a little to pretend they did.'

'So you dealt with your correspondence, sir, and then went to
your filing-cabinet?'

'That's right. I thought it ought to be on record that those girls
had left. I mean, it would look very odd if they were — if they had
a road accident in, say, Cornwall, when they were supposed to be
on holiday up here. Well, of course, when I looked for the file on
Cabin Eight it wasn't there.'

'Was that the only file which was missing?'

'No. Several others had gone, and that one was among them. All the missing files were under the initial L.'

'L could be for Lestrange or for Lyndhurst. That might be significant. Well, I'm glad you reported this, sir. It may help us. As soon as Constable March has finished, perhaps you will permit me to inspect one or two of the files which are left.'

'You think my loss may tie up with the theft at the hostel?'

'I don't think anything at the moment, sir. I am still collecting what evidence I can.'

'You don't mean that this ties up with the murders, do you? I have had three cancellations of late autumn bookings already.'

'I don't think anything and I don't mean anything. Finished, March? Right, then. By your leave, sir.' He went over to the filing-cabinet.

He was patient and thorough. It had occurred to him that L also stood for Lindsay. Only the L files were missing.

'The interesting thing is, ma'am,' said Ribble, 'that one missing file was that of the cabin which the forest warden had let to the four young ladies.'

'Are the files comprehensive?'

'How do you mean, ma'am?'

'Do they list the names and addresses of all the occupants of a cabin, or do they show only the name of the person who made the booking?'

'Oh, this warden is very conscientious indeed, ma'am. The name and address of the person who booked is on the file, and marked with a red asterisk, but also on the record are the names and addresses of the other tenants. As he explained to me, he cannot be too careful, as the tenants are not covered by insurance so far as the Forestry Commission is concerned, so he feels personally responsible for the safety of every one of them. Of course, family parties (which he says a great many of them are) go down under the name of the husband and under his address, and the rest is written off as Mrs Whatever-the-Name-Is and the number of children, but if it's a mixed party or a male or female party of adults, all the names go down and any addresses which are different from the address of the person who makes the booking.'

'The system sounds very thorough.'

'Well, ma'am, when you multiply the number of cabins with a possible five or even six people in each, he's responsible for a fair number of holidaymakers. I shall be interested to see whether the dabs from the hostel and the dabs from the filing-cabinet can tell us anything. I took the precaution of fingerprinting the dancers before I let them go.'

'You shall pursue the dabs; I will become a dabbler,' said Dame Beatrice.

'Ma'am?'

'I propose to roam the wild wet woods in search of *Amanita phalloides*.'

'Ah, this death-cap toad-stool the murderer seems so fond of.'

'To sum it up in those words seems to suggest that he might choose to eat it, in which case our hunt would not be up, but over. It is a little late in the season to find this particular fungus, but, as the murderer seems to have access to it, there must be some specimens about.'

She set out, accompanied by Laura.

'I suppose I mustn't ask any why or wherefore?' said the latter, when they reached the entrance to the forest.

'Better not. Can you keep the car down to about twenty-five miles an hour, stopping now and then, opening the bonnet and affecting to tinker with the engine? I want to give somebody a chance to catch up with us and pass us.'

'I should think they would be glad of the chance if I'm to drive so slowly. I'm consumed with curiosity, needless to say. Are we being pursued by wicked men? Is my wallet safe? — not that there's very much in it.'

'There was a tandem parked outside the Ewe and Lamb.'

'Couldn't be *the* tandem, could it? That one must have been jettisoned miles away from here.'

'One would suppose so, but a means of transport is a means of transport and not (except in gangster films) an amenity which is too readily sacrificed. Besides, what you so rightly distinguish as *the* tandem is the last thing the police will be expecting to find so near Gledge End, from which it disappeared. A bold bluff pays off more often than not.'

'But what makes the connection in your mind?'

'Only the presence of a tandem outside the Ewe and Lamb. I think I am being kept under observation.'

'I don't like the sound of that. Two women have been killed already.'

'For a reason which would not apply to me.'

Several cars passed them when Laura stopped and opened the bonnet. Dame Beatrice, apparently interested only in watching Laura's tinkering, noted with satisfaction that a tandem, with a man and a girl on it, both pedalling furiously, shot past only about a quarter of a mile from the forest carpark.

'Come out from there,' she said, 'and full speed ahead.' When Laura had parked the car, Dame Beatrice approached a boy who was eating potato crisps.

'You wouldn't have seen my nephew and his wife get off a tandem just now?' she said. The boy pointed.

'They went that way,' he said.

'Thank you. Come, Laura, perhaps we can catch up with them.'

'Easy,' said the boy. 'They weren't hurrying.'

Dame Beatrice and Laura turned into one of the forest 'rides' and found it bordered and sheltered by a big plantation of larches. Most of the foliage had been shed. Only the fir-cones remained on many of the trees.

Dame Beatrice stopped and addressed one of them, observing that she regretted her lack of interest in *Larix decidua*, but assuring the tree that this was only a temporary matter.

'What we are looking for,' she said, 'is a group of *Fagus sylvatica* or possibly *Quercus rober*.' She spoke loudly.

'I doubt whether we shall find beeches in these parts,' said Laura, 'but oaks ought to be fairly plentiful. The foresters must have planted hardwood trees as well as the pines and larches.'

A little further on its downward-sloping way the narrow

woodland road came out into a clearing. Standing in the middle of it were a noticeably sturdy young man and a plump young woman. They were looking at a solitary sheep which was standing beside a little, boulder-strewn stream. Dame Beatrice, followed by Laura, walked up to the group.

'I wonder,' she said, 'whether you can help me.'

'Try us,' said the girl. 'Have you lost your way?'

'No, not our way, but our objective. We are looking for oak trees. We are informed that a variety of the edible fungus allied to the common mushroom, the wood-mushroom, can be found growing beneath them.'

'That's right,' said the young man. 'Cross the beck and follow the path uphill. We'll show you the way, if you like. Mind you don't slip on the stones.'

Less than fifteen minues brought the party to a noble grove of oaks. Under the trees there appeared to be two species of fungi. Dame Beatrice pointed this out.

'I wonder which is the species we want? The two kinds look much alike to the untrained eye,' she said.

'Yes, you want to be careful,' said the man.

'Personally, you won't catch me eating any of the nasty things,' said the young woman. 'I don't take any risks of *that* sort, thank you.'

'Oh, nonsense, Marion,' said her companion. 'You just have to learn to distinguish the edible kind from the rest.' He stooped and picked up an appetising-looking specimen which had a yellowish cap and as he pressed it in his hand it gave out a smell reminiscent of anise. 'This is the chap you've got to avoid,' he said. 'These,' 'he pointed to a yellowish-green specimen not unlike the other, 'are what you're after.'

'Really?' said Dame Beatrice. 'How deceptive Nature can be. If you had not told me, I should have thought it was the other way round.'

'Well, it isn't.' He flung down the squashed mess over which his hand had closed, went down to the beck and, kneeling, washed his hand in the clear, brown, ice-cold water and dried it on his handkerchief. 'If you ate any of those,' he said, 'you'd be dead in twelve hours, but the other kind are all right. Oh, well — but you haven't got a basket. How are you going to carry your mushrooms home?'

Laura unfastened the headscarf she was wearing.

'This will do,' she said. 'Thanks a lot.'

'Don't mention it. Well, we'll be getting along.' The two of them walked on and the grove of oaks was very quiet, for the wind scarcely moved the age-old, mighty boughs. Neither Dame Beatrice nor Laura said a word until they had remained for a few moments looking down at the fungi, and then had crossed the beck. Laura spoke first.

'Well,' she said, 'what did you make of those two?'

'If such a remark were not *tabu* in these enlightened days, I should say that they hardly seem to come from the same social stratum.'

'Yes, but — I mean, the information!'

'Yes, indeed. I was afraid you were going to spoil the fun.'

'I definitely would have spoken up if I didn't know that you'd done your homework, both as a doctor and a criminologist, on the subject of fungi in general and the poisonous kinds in particular. But didn't you yourself want to contradict him? I mean, if he's going about telling people to eat that deadly stuff, he's going to have somebody else's death on his hands. I take it he is the chap the police are after.'

'The general description would fit and undoubtedly he hardly wishes us well.'

'What shall you do about him?'

'Describe the encounter to Inspector Ribble, but it will lead to nothing until we have proof that this man is the murderer, and, so far, we have no proof of that.'

'But he's done his best to ensure that we eat deadly poisonous toadstools.'

'Yes, he is puffed up with his own conceit, and is becoming reckless. He will soon go too far.'

# —16—

# WITCHES' FINGERS

'Well, we can both give a pretty accurate description of the chap,' said Laura, 'but I suppose Ribble can hardly arrest him on a charge of mistaking a deadly poisonous *Amanita* for a harmless, delicious *Agaricus*, can he?'

'Someone else appears to have done some homework! No, of course he cannot, especially as the two species can be confused quite innocently.'

'If you are right, what about that girl he had with him? Isn't she in the most frightful danger?'

'Up to the present she is in no danger at all.'

'Just because she doesn't happen to be one of the dancers?'

'That is not the reason. Do not tantalise yourself with these speculations. The person I am most anxious about *is* one of the dancers, however. It is the girl they call Pippa. I also feel concern for the younger Miss Lindsay, but Miss Erica Lyndhurst has been warned. I am thankful that those four young women are getting together again and that my nephew Carey's farm is a very long way from the murderer's sphere of activities. Tamsin would be perfectly safe there except for one thing.'

'Let me guess. Those stolen records, the one from the Youth Hostel and the set from the forest office, contain the home addresses of all the people concerned.'

'Yes, including that of the murderer. Fortunately Inspector

Ribble has listed the hostel addresses in the notes he gave me, so we have that much help.'

'Will it be sufficient?'

'Unless the murderer gave a false address. It is quite likely that he did. It is a pity that Hermione's home address was on record in the files stolen from the forest warden, but, as I say, Stanton St John is a long way from here.'

'The murderer wouldn't know that the girls have gone there.'

'It may not take him long to find out. He has all their home addresses.'

'Is Hermione herself in any danger?'

'All four girls are in *some* danger, perhaps. That depends upon how far our murderer is prepared to go; but the greatest danger is to Miss Tamsin Lindsay. When I have done what still remains to be done here, I shall make it my business to go to the farm and keep an eye on things.'

'I don't see what else can be done here that Ribble can't do.'

'Well, perhaps not *here*, exactly. It is very fortunate that I was able to see Mrs Beck's register before it was stolen.'

'I thought you got the dancers' addresses from Ribble. You didn't need —'

'Oh, I like to check my information,' said Dame Beatrice airily. 'To add to yours, I will disclose to you all my suspicions and my reasons for them, but, until today's encounter, I had nothing to go on except applied psychology.'

'Where is our next assignment? — and with whom?'

'The inquest on Miss Peggy Raincliffe is to be held at Gledge End tomorrow. I am anxious to hear the medical evidence. After that, I hope to be allowed to talk to young Mr Marton before we go to Stanton St John.'

'Meanwhile, what about this girl Pippa?'

'She is under police protection and Inspector Ribble has promised me that she will be extremely well-guarded until the murderer is caught. There is nothing more that she can tell us, although I may perhaps go to see her at her home.'

'Surely she's got *some* suspicions of who killed the other girls and attacked her brother?'

'Except for her music, she is an exceptionally imperceptive child, I think.'

'Well, I'm all agog for information. Who dunnit?'

Dame Beatrice told her, but added, 'There isn't an atom of proof, of course, that would stand up to lawyers' arguments.'

The coroner sat with a full complement of jurors, seven men and four women, and he explained to them that he could accept a majority verdict provided that not more than two of them dissented from it.

'So nine of you have to be agreed,' he said, stressing his point. 'This is not a trial, I would have you remember. It is an enquiry into the cause of death, when and at what place death occurred, and whether the deceased has been formally identified and by whom. You are permitted to ask questions of the witness, but I shall rule out any queries which I deem to be irrelevant or in any way mischievous. You are to find your verdict purely on the evidence that you will hear, putting out of your minds any rumours, gossip or slander which may have come to your ears.'

Having done his best to cow them and added the further warning that he had power to override their verdict if he did not agree with it, he opened the proceedings by calling for the identification of the body. This was sworn to by the mother of the deceased, and the medical evidence followed.

Death had been assured by one heavy blow in the centre of the forehead which had rendered the victim unconscious and which could not have been self-inflicted. It was followed by other assaults after she had fallen down. There were more blows to the back of the head which would have caused death. The weapon had probably been a heavy stone with a rough surface.

Inspector Ribble was called. He said that he had been asked to go to St Vortigern's Church Hall as there had been an accident. When he arrived he was shewn two bodies, one still alive, the other dead.

'Who telephoned you?' asked the coroner.

'William Dexter, the caretaker at the church hall. He had also telephoned for a doctor.'

When the caretaker was called he made as good and as laconic a witness as the inspector had done, having forgotten none of his training as a policeman in the art of giving evidence in court. All the same, his story took some time to tell, as the corner asked for a good many details.

'You knew nothing of what had happened until you went to your broom-cupboard?'

'Not a thing, sir.'

'Did nothing strike you as being out of the ordinary?'

'Yes, sir. I noticed, soon as I went in, that the back door was wide open.'

'Was that unusual?'

'Most unusual, being that it's always kept bolted on the inside.'

'Why is that?'

'We get tramps, sir, and boys up to mischief. There's a fair bit of waste ground outside that door. There's trees and bushes.'

'To whom does it belong?'

'I reckon it belongs to the hall, sir, but nobody tends it and children use it as a playgound. If I left the back door of the hall unlocked, tramps might use that room as a doss-down or boys could get in and do damage. It's happened, sir, so I had vicar order the bolts to be put on. The window is too high up to be reached without a ladder, and the little window in the washroom adjoining is too small even for a thin boy to get through, so vicar and me have found the bolts quite adequate.'

'But not on this occasion.'

'One of the party as hired the hall opened the door from the inside — must have done, sir. There's no other way.'

'Well, as whoever did that is not present . . .'

'No, he's in hospital and won't be available yet for questioning,' said Ribble from his seat.

'Thank you, Inspector.' The coroner turned again to the witness. 'After you had found the deceased's body . . .'

'That there body found *him*, as I understand it,' put in a juryman.

'Just so. The point is immaterial.'

'Begging your leave, it ent nothing of sort. Ask him how long that corpse would have stayed in cupboard if he hadn't happened to go to it for his broom.'

'Well, Dexter, you may answer the question,' said the coroner.

'I reckon it would have stayed there till Wednesday, when I should have needed my broom to sweep the hall for the Women's Institute Keep Fit, them doing some of their exercise laying on the floor. The hall wasn't let to any outsiders this week, so I could make one sweep-up sufficient.'

'Sufficient for several days?' asked a woman juror.

'I don't sweep up after the Saturday Youth Club, the man that runs it being an ex-sergeant who don't allow smoking nor litter, and, if the hall ent let, there's no need to sweep up after the Sunday school until the W.I.'s on Wednesday. Then it does again until the Saturday, those being my orders and by arrangement with the churchwardens.'

'Well, your question seems to have been relevant, after all,' said the coroner to the juror. 'Now, Dexter, how did you come to discover the injured man?'

'When I went to close the back door, sir, thinking it unwise to leave it open, I saw his foot sticking out from under a bush on that bit of waste ground I mentioned. Then I phoned about him and the body.'

'You seem to have acted very promptly and sensibly all through. Well, I think we have heard enough. The jury may consider their verdict.'

'Person or persons unknown,' said Ribble to Dame Beatrice, when they had left the court. 'Unanimous, too, as it could hardly fail to be. I thought that one or two of them would have liked to ask something more about this boy who's in hospital. I'm applying again for permission to question him. I've seen him, but they wouldn't let me stay. He doesn't know yet that the girl is dead. That will have to be broken to him because he will have to give evidence when the inquest is resumed. I hope you will accompany me, ma'am, when I go to see him. What he has to say may help to prove whether your ideas are right. I still have a kind of liking for my own.'

The meeting with the injured boy took place on that same afternoon. Mick was sitting up and smiled when he saw them.

'Does this mean I can get out of this place?' he asked. 'I'm perfectly all right, you know.'

'You won't be here much longer, I'm sure, sir. You know who I am, don't you?'

'I haven't lost my memory. Have you come to grill me again?'

'Just to put a few questions. This is Dame Beatrice Lestrange Bradley.'

'Good Lord! They haven't told you I'm crazy, have they? Have I been babbling while I was unconscious? You have to get *two* doctors, don't you? I know Dame Beatrice is a *supremo*, but —'

'Calm yourself,' said Dame Beatrice. 'I am not here as a psychiatrist, but as one who is deeply concerned to prove the identity of the person who attacked you and who killed Mrs Tyne.'

'And you and Mrs Tyne are not his only victims,' said Ribble, 'so tell us everything you know. First, did you know that Miss Peggy Raincliffe followed you into the changing-room?'

'Trust *her*! She *would*!'

'Steady on with your strictures, sir. I am afraid she pursued you once too often. The poor young lady is dead . . . Take it easy, sir. I thought you might have guessed.'

'I had no idea, of course I hadn't! All I know is that I opened the back door and went outside to get a breath of air. Besides, I thought I heard somebody knock.'

'This was after you had changed your dance costume at the end of the show?'

'Yes. The sword-dance team, with me in my whites and that stinking beard, had been photographed, and then they wanted a picture of the other dancers. Well, the other men didn't have to change because they had kept on most of the morris gear for the last item — it's a sword-dance, as I said — and Peggy didn't have to change, either, because she played for the last item, she didn't dance in it, so that only left me. Well, I changed in the washroom and then opened the door and just stepped out into that shrubbery bit, and before I knew anything about it, some frightful lout must have come up behind me and hit me over the head.'

'And that is really all you remember, sir?'

'Of course it is. I say, tell me about Peggy, will you?'

'You were a long time gone, sir, so I understand that she volunteered, in an impetuous manner which forestalled anybody else among your company, to go into the changing-room to hurry you up. We think she must have been a witness to the assault on you.'

'And this crazy devil turned on her . . .'

'That is about the size of it, sir. He dared not leave her alive when he knew she had seen him.'

'But why should the fellow want to attack *me*?'

'We think that, once you had changed your clothes for the last photograph, he mistook you for your sister,' said Dame Beatrice.

'But why should he knock on the door?'

'Well, sir,' said Ribble, 'if Dame Beatrice is right, he must have seen you through the window when you came out of the washroom.'

'The window is too high up.'

'Too high up for anybody to get in by without a ladder, yes, sir.'

'But not so high up that a lissom person could not leap up and take a look at the room,' said Dame Beatrice. 'He probably heard you moving about and was actuated at first simply out of curiosity. When he saw what he thought was your sister who, so far as he knew, had no reason to suspect him of evil intentions, he knocked on the door which, for your own reasons, you had already decided to open.'

'But why didn't I see him?'

'He had already taken cover.'

'But what did he have against Pippa? — that is, if he mistook me for her.'

'A deep wound to his vanity,' said Dame Beatrice.

'But what about Judy? Why was she killed that day on the moors?'

'The inference is that he met her, waylaid her and was repulsed, as your sister repulsed him. Mrs Tyne did not want his company, I think. He then knocked her off her bicycle and assaulted her, an assault which ended in her death. We shall never prove this, but it is a tenable hypothesis.'

'But, if you know all this, why can't you arrest him?'

'Because, as Dame Beatrice says, we have no proof,' said Ribble.

'Oh, Lord! If only I hadn't opened that damned back door!'

'No need to blame yourself,' said Dame Beatrice briskly. 'You could not possibly have known that anybody would attack you or Miss Raincliffe.'

'Granted that your theories about the murderer are right, ma'am,' said Ribble, when they had left the hospital, 'why *was* the murderer lurking? If he had it in mind to kill Miss Pippa, whom her brother so closely resembles, he must have known or found out that the back door was kept bolted. Why was he round there at all?'

'Oh, Inspector, what a question! He was not there with intent to commit murder, but to carry out a natural function which the screening bushes made possible. It was when he had fulfilled his perfectly innocent purpose that he heard sounds from inside, leapt up to glance in at the window and saw (as he thought) Miss Pippa. The opportunity thus fortuitously offered him was too good to let slip. He had intended to follow her up and kill her at some time, in any case. Mr Marton's very thick wig and Miss Raincliffe's sudden appearance saved one life but destroyed the other.'

'The other dancers would have known of Mr Marton's claustrophobia, you know, ma'am.'

'I see what you mean, Inspector.'

'One, in particular, being closest to him, would have counted on him opening that back door when he found himself shut up alone in that changing-room with no window it was possible for him to open. What was to stop this man from slipping out of the main door while the rest of them were chatting with the photographer? It wouldn't take him a minute to nip round the building, and Mr Marton would probably have recognised his knock on the door, but isn't going to incriminate him.'

Dame Beatrice shook her head.

'You are forgetting the tandem,' she pointed out. 'It had disappeared. That means that it was probably cycled on to the moor and hidden there. No member of the dance company could have been absent long enough to have carried out such an operation. Oh, no, Inspector, your theory will not hold water. Mr Nicolson is not our murderer.'

'There's the psychological angle, as you yourself agree, ma'am. In other words, I reckon Mr Nicolson had a stronger motive for murdering those two girls than anybody else we've considered. They were a menace, as I see it, to what might be called by some "a beautiful friendship".'

'But we've discussed that aspect. It does not account for the vicious attack on Mr Marton himself.'

'Punishment for stepping out of line? Jealousy is a strange force, ma'am. That also we've discussed.'

'Why do you suppose Mrs Beck's records were stolen? That also we have talked about. You think they were taken as a blind, don't you? I say that the murderer needed them because he did not know the home address of Miss Marton, and that he took the records from the forest warden's filing cabinet because he did not know the home address of Tamsin Lindsay, or where the other girls live.'

Ribble spread out his hands.

'I grant everything you say, ma'am,' he admitted, 'but my theory seems so much more *likely* than yours, if you'll allow me to say so. Look, you say your man is still in the neighbourhood and you met him in the forest. Suppose I pull him in and question him? I can't hold him, but his answers might give me a line. Why, in any case, should he have stolen the tandem? One of the bicycles would have been far easier for him to manage and much less noticeable on the road. And who's to say whether the tandem was ever put into that shed at the church hall at all? I don't suppose all the dancers turned their bikes in at exactly the same time.'

'Mr Marton would have known if the tandem had been left in some other place.'

'It wouldn't have been any use him knowing if Mr Nicolson

murdered him. I've convinced myself that the attack on Mr Marton was with murderous intent, ma'am, and that Nicolson's plan was to hide the tandem so as to make it look as though Mr Marton and Miss Raincliffe had gone away on it at the end of the show. According to what the caretaker told me, that's what the others *did* think until the truth came out. We were told by his sister that Marton is weak and impressionable. It would have been easy enough, it seems to me, for Nicolson to have given Marton some reason or other as to why they shouldn't leave the tandem with the other bikes in that shed.'

'Your reasoning is valid up to a point, and I think you might be justified in arresting Mr Nicolson on the strength of it, but only if Mr Marton were dead, Mr Marton is very much alive and could refute your theory about the tandem as soon as the defending lawyer had put him in the witness box.'

'The prosecution would claim that he was still under Nicolson's influence, ma'am, and was unwilling to denounce his friend. Anyway, I shall have another go at Marton as soon as he can be discharged from hospital. I am impressed by your ideas, ma'am. It's only that I prefer my own.'

'As who would not?' said Dame Beatrice cordially. 'Nevertheless, Inspector, I'll take the high road and you'll take the low road (or *vice versa*, of course — the choice is yours) and I have a feeling that I'll be in Scotland before you.'

'There's always the story of the hare and the tortoise, ma'am.'

'I know; but which of us is which?'

'Do you really believe Ribble will arrest Nicolson?' asked Laura. Dame Beatrice cackled.

'Oh, no,' she said. 'Inspector Ribble knows perfectly well that he has no case against Mr Nicolson. He was enjoying himself by arguing with me, that is all. On the other hand, neither have *I* a case which, at present, would survive examination. Our next excursion, yours and mine, is to Long Cove Bay.'

'That hostel again?'

'No. We are going to visit a public house.'

'Good-o, but why?'

'You may know when we get there, but I can promise nothing. This really *will* be a shot in the dark. If it finds its mark it will be because of the notes of his own painstaking work with which the inspector provided me, and I shall take pleasure in saying as much, both to him and to his Chief Constable.'

'So he doesn't mean to arrest our nominee either?'

'Good gracious, no. That was a probe to find out whether I know something I have not told him. It failed because I have disclosed to him all that is in my heart concerning this affair.'

'But he thinks it's weak on motive. Is the motive he assigns to Nicolson any stronger?'

'A policeman would think so, I daresay. There is considerable bias about *some* relationships.'

# –17–

# DESTROYING ANGEL

Hermione, sure of her road, brought Isobel by way of High Wycombe, skirted Wheatley and then took the minor road north-westward through Forest Hill and so to her home. Erica and Tamsin, in Erica's car, arrived an hour later, and all were soon at table.

'So you've been having adventures,' said Jenny, their hostess.

'What has Aunt Adela been up to?' asked Carey. 'You say she sent you away from the forest area.'

'She thought we might be murdered if we stayed, so Isobel took me to her London flat and Erica took Tamsin home with her, and then I got this idea of all of us coming down here. The two working women have to go back on Saturday afternoon, but Tamsin can stay on for a bit. She wants to draw pigs. You might like to have a portrait of Lucifer,' said Hermione to her father.

'Is Lucifer a pig?' asked Tamsin.

'He's my prize boar,' Carey replied. 'You shall see him tomorrow. We call him Lucifer, but his name, when I show him, is Harold Longtooth of Roman Ending. There's a Roman villa not too far away and I bought the farm which is next door to it and added it to my own. I've built my pigman a cottage out there and pulled the old farmhouse down. It was a bit of an eyesore, anyway.'

'Would you really let me paint Harold? I've sketched dogs, but never a boar. And are there woods on your estate?'

'I expect you miss the forest,' said Jenny, 'but we do have woods near by. We don't own them, but we have rights of pannage, so, if any of you are short of something to do while you're here, you can always go and gather acorns and beech-mast. The pigs love both, and I can supply baskets and clean sacks. Pigs are forest animals. Of course nowadays we don't let them loose in the woods, which is what they would enjoy most, but we keep them in pig-houses with a shed and a large outside run, so I think they are fairly happy, especially as they've never known anything else. The pig-houses are a good way off, but Carey will trundle you round in the jeep and you can easily get to the woods from there.'

'I hope Aunt Adela isn't in danger of being murdered,' said Carey, who had not taken the possibility seriously.

'She told me she would still have Laura and Detective-Inspector Ribble with her,' Hermione replied, 'so she ought to be all right. In any case the murderer only specialises in young women. That's why Tamsin is such a responsibility.'

'What about you?' retorted Tamsin. 'Anyway, it is all to do with those dance people. None of us was in any danger.'

'Then why was Dame Beatrice so anxious that we shouldn't let anybody know where we were going?' asked Isobel, looking at Erica.

'Oh, it is a precautionary measure,' Erica replied, 'but she was insistent about our leaving the forest cabin, so I felt I had to agree. After all, two girls have been killed. She was right to make us leave.'

'Oh, well, nobody knows where we are except for Mr and Mrs Lestrange and my mother,' said Tamsin. 'I thought somebody in the family ought to be told where we were.'

'Quite right,' said Jenny. 'I should always want to know where Hermy was.'

' "That old-fashioned mother of mine!" ' chanted Hermione. 'You are way, way behind the times, darling! Parents never want to know what their children are up to nowadays in case somebody holds them responsible for whatever it is.'

'If only the parents *were* held responsible there would be a lot less truancy in schools and far better behaviour all round,' said Isobel severely. 'As for this nonsense that a child of under ten is incapable of committing any crime, I never heard such rubbish in my life. I could tell you —'

'Oh, head her off, somebody!' said Tamsin. 'You shouldn't talk shop, Isobel, especially at table.'

'Oh, oh!' said Erica. 'Is this a case of the bunny biting the stoat? What have *you* been up to that you turn so belligerent all of a sudden?'

'I haven't been up to anything. Of course I haven't. What *should* I have been up to?'

' "Methinks the lady doth protest too much",' said Hermione. 'Come clean, young Tamsin. You've given somebody else this address, haven't you?'

'Well, only John,' admitted Tamsin, 'and that can't possibly hurt. He won't pass it on, I'm sure. He would hate not to know where I am.'

' "Kind hearts are more than coronets And simple faith than Norman blood," ' said her sister. 'What a priceless fathead you can be when you really make up your mind to it!'

'So we visit another pub,' said Laura, 'but why George? I could have driven the car. Do we need a bodyguard?'

'We may have to park outside a house while we conduct what I think will be our last interview. As I have a feeling that a back street in Long Cove Bay may not be the safest place to leave an unattended car, I decided to bring George along,' Dame Beatrice explained.

'I see. So the visit to the pub is not the only reason for our taking this trip across the moors.'

On their right they were passing a pine-forest which looked almost black because of its density. On their left, dreary with faded heather and sad, although colourful, with acres of gold, dead bracken, the moors rose in the distance in folds of blue, grey and dirty green, a mysterious, monotonous, nostalgic, tragic landscape, while ahead of the car there stretched, wound, mounted and fell the apparently endless ribbon of moorland road snaking its way towards the world's end. Laura summed up the landscape.

'Enough to give you the willies,' she said. As the car approached Long Cove Bay the road began to descend, but very gradually and then it turned to the right, past the Youth Hostel, and made for the town.

Ribble had served Dame Beatrice well. He had named the pub in his notes and had given the address to which he had taken the girl, whose name he could give only as Marion. He had added a footnote to the effect that she had been of no help to him.

The pub was small, cosy and not particularly busy, as it was past one o'clock and its habitués had gone home or to cafés for their midday meal. Laura ordered ham sandwiches and beer for herself and George, a cheese sandwich and sherry for Dame Beatrice and then, going to the counter for a second round of drinks, she mentioned Marion's name.

'You know her?' asked the barmaid.

'Mutual friends,' said Laura, 'asked me to look her up. Is she working?'

'Her? Not bloody likely!' said the barmaid. 'What, with the Welfare only too ready and willing? I wouldn't work, either, if I could stick being at home all day with my old man, but I can't. One thing about this job, you've always got company and you don't have to fork out for their nosh.'

'You don't come from these parts,' said Laura. 'Neither do I. Good old London! Is Marion likely to be in this morning?'

Correctly interpreting this, the barmaid replied that Marion would not be in until the evening for her 'usual' and that she and the barmaid were going out that afternoon window-shopping in Gledge End.

'Marion can borrow the tandem,' she said. 'on account her boyfriend has got to go to Birmingham on business by train.'

Laura returned to the table at which she had left Dame Beatrice and communicated these tidings to her. Dame Beatrice made no comment, but as soon as Laura had drunk her second half-pint she led the way out and went straight to a public call-box from which she rang Detective-Inspector Ribble, told him where he could find a tandem, and suggested that it might be the one stolen from the church hall.

'It's the right tandem,' said Ribble on the following day. 'Right make, right colour, right lamps, right accessories, as described to us by young Marton. I was allowed in to see him again. He expects to be discharged from hospital in a day or two, but, except for the description of the tandem, about which he was very clear — he and Nicolson appear to cherish the thing the same way as some young men cherish a sports car — he couldn't help me any further. Still has no idea who his assailant was and remembers nothing of Miss Raincliffe's bursting into the room. I suppose he'd just been knocked unconscious when she arrived on the scene. Anyway, we'll pick up our chap for the theft of the tandem. We can hold him for that and, as there is this more serious charge of murder in the offing, we shall be fully justified in opposing bail.'

'I don't think you need waste the time of the Birmingham police,' said Dame Beatrice. 'If I read his mind aright, the most likely place to find him will be in or near the village of Stanton St John. He will have found out by this time that his next victim (as he supposes) is not at her home address.'

'If you're right about the motive for the murder of Mrs Tyne and the murderous attack on Mr Marton, I think you're right about Stanton St John, ma'am. As you indicated, why else would the forest warden's records have been stolen?'

'So you have come round to my point of view.'

'He must be pretty reckless to have stuck to the tandem. He must have known it would be recognised sooner or later,' said Ribble.

'He may have felt safe at first when he knew you had rounded up the dancers and placed them in a position which approximated to their being held in custody. As soon as he found out that you had let them go, he co-opted this girl Marion, thinking that nobody would be looking for *two* people on the tandem.'

'I suppose she is in no danger from him?'

'None at all, unless she wounds his *amour propre*, and from what I saw of the two of them in the forest clearing, there is little chance of that at present.'

'We used to have a marvellous cook who was also quite a character,' said Jenny to Erica. 'Her name was Mrs Ditch. Of course she's been dead for some years now, but we still have her son, known to all as Our Walt. He is Carey's pig-man now and has three underlings to whom he acts as a benevolent despot. I don't know what we should do without him.He's a first-class handyman as well. His wife is the present cook and she's good, too.'

'I wish she would show me how to make a bacon pudding and how to do pig's fry.'

'She'll be delighted to, if you ask her. What about her recipe for black pluddings? What are the others doing this morning? I haven't seen them since breakfast.'

'Isobel needed exercise and has walked to Oxford. She said she might do some shopping. I expect that means she'll look at the University booksellers and take a taxi back here to be in time for lunch. You said it would not be until two, so she thought she would have time. She'll be back all right. She isn't scatty, like young Tamsin. Tamsin is sketching pigs.'

'I hope she is well wrapped up. It's a bit chilly sitting about at this time of year.'

'Oh, yes, she's got a windcheater and a scarf. She'll be all right. Hermione is more or less with her.'

'Only more or less?'

'I think she said she was going the rounds with Our Walt.'

'I didn't intend her to start work again while you three girls were here. Carey has gone to Oxford, too. I want some household things and he's ordering feed, so I thought he could combine the two. If only he had known, he could have taken Isobel in the car.'

'Oh, she wanted to walk. Perhaps they will meet and he will bring her back. I think I'll take a stroll myself and see how Tamsin is getting on.'

'Are you worried about yourself and the others? What did Aunt Adela tell you? She telephoned me, you know, when she heard from Hermy that you were all coming here to finish your holiday.'

'She told me that we weren't safe so long as we stayed in the

forest cabin. She said she thought Tamsin was the most vulnerable, Isobel the least, and Hermione in less danger than myself.
She told us all not to trust anybody we had met while we were in
the forest and, except that I don't scare easily, she would have had
me scared, because, of course, we did get well acquainted with a
hefty young man named John Trent, who seemed rather
interested in young Tamsin.'

'Aunt Adela did not name any particular person, though, did
she?'

'Well, yes, she did, but it seems so improbable that he could be
a danger to any of us. The only ones who seem to have upset him
are a company of folk-dance people. They are the ones he seems
to have it in for, not us.'

'If Aunt Adela said that you four were in danger, she meant it,'
said Jenny. 'You say that Isobel is not particularly vulnerable, but
ought she to have walked into Oxford alone?'

'You can't argue with Isobel and she's very sensible. She'll be
all right once she gets to Headington. That's the way she was
going to take. It's about five miles, she thought, to get right into
the city.'

At this point, before the conversation could continue, Our
Walt's wife appeared.

'The poultry be at the door, missus, and want to know what
about a fowl for Sunday, loike.'

'We shall need two, Mrs Ditch. I'd better see him.' She went
out to the back door and Erica followed her plan of going out to
see how Tamsin was progressing with her pencil sketches of the
pigs.

She found the youngest member of their party outside
Lucifer's pen. Tamsin looked round and said, 'He won't keep still
long enough for me to draw him properly. I think he can smell one
of the sows.'

'He's not supposed to be able to,' said Hermione, coming up to
them. 'He probably objects to an alien presence and perhaps he's
got a "thing" about having a picture made of himself. Boars are
very primitive, I always think, unlike sows and young pigs, who
are very intelligent and good-humoured. Did you ever see a pig
smile? They do, you know, *and* they can say "Thank you" when

you feed them. Think of Empress of Blandings when some kind person picked up a potato she'd dislodged and returned it to her trough. Why don't you let Lucifer settle down a bit and go and sketch Sunspot?'

'Which is Sunspot?'

'She is that lovely Gloucester Old Spot over there. She's only a young gilt and hasn't farrowed yet. She's as docile as a pet dog. We are thinking of breeding Gloucesters.'

'Do you really *like* pigs, Hermy?' asked Tamsin, accompanying her friend across the rough grass.

'Love them. They're clean and they've got such a sense of humour. Besides, I was brought up with them.'

She saw Tamsin settled and watched the first confident strokes of the pencil. Sunspot came to the front of the sizeable wired pen, looked enquiringly at Tamsin and Hermione through the meshes and then went to the wooden gate through which she was sometimes allowed to pass while her domain was mucked out. On these occasions she was kept happy and from straying by the present of a succulent cabbage or some other interesting tit-bit and for some reason she seemed to think that Tamsin's activities promised something pleasant of this nature. She scrabbled at the woodwork with her little front trotters and made pleading little anticipatory grunts, snorts and snuffles.

Tamsin got up from her stool and looked over the four-foot door which was hung between two higher iron posts.

'I can't sketch you if you're going to stay there,' she protested. Hermione laughed and said that she would go and get the pig an apple. Erica volunteered to accompany her and as they made towards the house the pigmen joined them to go in for their mid-morning snack. At the same time as they and the girls disappeared, a young man came out of the woods and walked up a miry but well-marked path which led to a five-barred gate in a wired-up hedge. The gate and hedge marked Carey's boundaries on that side of the pig-farm.

The man stood looking over the gate for some minutes, but as soon as the coast was clear, with Hermione, Erica and the pigmen out of sight, he climbed over the gate. Tamsin, who was completely absorbed in looking over the top of Sunspot's gate and trying to cajole that engaging animal into going into the open run, was surprised, but not startled, to hear a shout of 'Hi!' She turned to see Adam Penshaw coming towards her. Her first feeling was one of disappointment. She had been hoping for John Trent to come and look them up. She was pretty sure that, when he found she was not in her own home, he would have got the Oxfordshire address from her mother.

When she recognised Adam her reaction was one of anger. It was intolerable that he was still determined to pester her. She shouted, 'Go away! You're trespassing!'

He continued to advance, calling out, 'Come for a walk in the woods. I want to talk to you!'

'Go away! You're being a nuisance,' she called back. He halted.

'I'm being *what*?' he shouted.

'A beastly nuisance! You're not wanted. Go away!'

'If you don't come I'll let all these pigs out!'

At this moment Hermione reappeared. She took in the situation in an instant and began to walk towards him. As she did so, he laughed and pushed back the bolt of the pig-pen on which he was leaning. Hermione turned and tore back towards where Tamsin was irresolutely standing.

'Quick, Tammie,' she yelled. 'Get over the door. Sunspot won't hurt you.' Tamsin accepted this reassurance and took the breathless advice, and Hermione tumbled over Sunspot's door almost on top of her. Sunspot, who had retired into the centre of her fenced enclosure in rational surprise at receiving this sudden and unexpected influx of visitors, stood regarding the heap of arms and legs before she retired to her covered shed, from the opening to which she poked out an enquiring snout.

Tamsin began to scramble to her feet, but Hermione pulled her down as a hoarse and terrible screaming broke out.

'You don't want to see what's happening,' she stammered. 'He's let out that devil Lucifer.'

'No suggestion that Lucifer should be put down,' said Carey, when the inquest on Adam Penshaw was concluded. 'The verdict was death by misadventure. There was a notice up beside the gate the lad came in by, and another notice beside the boar's pen.'

'You knew Adam was the murderer, didn't you?' said Hermione to her great-aunt. 'How long ago did you know it?'

'The various encounters you four girls had with him were pointers. After what he thought was a promising beginning, you all rejected him, and not only once. Then Miss Pippa rejected him that day at Ramsgill farm and at the hall he mistook her brother for her and did his best to kill the young man. Subsequently, of course, he learned from the newspapers that he had chosen the wrong victim. In the state of mind in which I judged him to be, it was inevitable that he would attempt to attack Miss Pippa again, but while she was under police protection he realised that this would be far too risky a proceeding. That turned his attention to his other objective, you four. At your first meeting you gave him a lift in your car. He had tricked you into doing this, his ego was satisfied and you, at that point, were safe.'

'He shouldn't have attempted to presume on the acquaintanceship,' said Hermione. 'He must have known that Tamsin and I were pretty sick with him for leading us up the garden so as to get a free ride to that Youth Hostel.'

'His natural conceit led him to take a chance, but after that you rejected him.'

'And John Trent threw him over our verandah railings,' said Erica. 'I wonder he didn't have a go at John. If it was rejection that upset him, well, nobody could have been more forcibly rejected than that.'

'Penshaw attacked only the unsuspecting, and even then they had to be weaker than himself,' said Dame Beatrice. 'Inspector Ribble would have got a conviction in due course, for Penshaw was becoming reckless. The girl Marion and her possession of the tandem almost clinched the matter. She had no reason to lie to the police on Penshaw's behalf. Well, I suppose it has been an interesting case, psychologically.'

'With a horrible ending,' said Tamsin, shuddering at the recollection of Adam Penshaw's screams.

'So did Judy Tyne and Peggy Raincliffe have a horrible ending. Don't forget that,' said Isobel.